THE OLD COUNTRY

MORDICAI GERSTEIN

THE OLD COUNTRY

ROARING BROOK PRESS
NEW MILFORD, CONNECTICUT

Copyright © 2005 by Mordicai Gerstein

Published by Roaring Brook Press

Roaring Brook Press is a division of Holtzbrinck Publishing Holdings Limited Partnership

143 West Street, New Milford, Connecticut 06776

Distributed in Canada by H. B. Fenn and Company Ltd.

Library of Congress Cataloging-in-Publication Data

Gerstein, Mordicai.

The Old Country / Mordicai Gerstein—1st ed.

p. cm.

ISBN-10: 1-59643-047-8   ISBN-13: 978-1-59643-047-1 (hardcover)

ISBN-10: 1-59643-192-x   ISBN-13: 978-1-59643-192-8 (paperback)

Summary: A grandmother tells her story of being tricked into exchanging her young body with that
of a fox and trying to get it back while a war tore apart her home and her country.

[1. Grandmothers—Fiction. 2. War—Fiction. 3. Foxes—Fiction.] I. Title.

PZ7.G325Ol 2005

[Fic]—dc22   2004023082

Roaring Brook Press books are available for special promotions and premiums.

For details contact: Director of Special Markets, Holtzbrinck Publishers.

Extract from Dry Loaf, by Wallace Stevens. From The Collected Poems of Wallace Stevens,
by Wallace Stevens, copyright © 1954 by Wallace Stevens and renewed 1982 by Holly Stevens.
Used by permission of Alfred A. Knopf, a division of Random House, Inc.

First edition May 2005

First paperback edition September 2006

Book design by Jennifer Browne

Printed in the United States of America

2 4 6 8 10 9 7 5 3 1 (hardcover)   2 4 6 8 10 9 7 5 3 1 (paperback)

For Lou Harris
with love

It was soldiers went marching over the rocks
And still the birds came, in watery flocks,
Because it was spring and the birds had to come.
No doubt that soldiers had to be marching
And that drums had to be rolling, rolling, rolling.

—Wallace Stevens

PRELUDE

❧ Great-Grandmother Gisella was from the Old Country, a country whose name and borders have changed so many times that no one knows anymore what it had been called originally. And though she left there in her early teens, and lived to well over ninety, or maybe even one hundred, she always wore the multicolored embroidered-felt clothes of her homeland, and her eyes never lost something of what I thought must be the light of the woods of that place. Even when I was very little, I thought there was something wild in the angle and expression of her golden eyes.

One Sunday afternoon, after a long train ride from her solitary old house in the mountains, she arrived laden with bags and bundles at our city apartment overlooking the great river.

Her face was walnut dark and wrinkled, and her golden eyes glittered with delight, as they always did, at the sight of me. I didn't know that this was the last time we would see each other.

She embraced me, and I felt the melted snowflakes on her cheek and smelled pine needles, maple-wood smoke, and hints of cinnamon, cardamom, and cumin, all of which, to me, were the smell of the mysterious Old Country.

She unloaded the bags she'd brought. There was, of course, her cinnamon honey cake and packages for my parents containing things her family had brought from the Old Country: rings and earrings, shawls, and faded photos in tarnished frames.

"And this," Great-Granny said to me, "is now yours." It was the battered old violin case I'd seen all my life. It was covered with travel stickers, and it contained the precious instrument she had played on concert stages all over the world. She had been a famous violinist until she retired in her eighties.

"You will make this old fiddle sing," she said to me. It was after dinner, and she was helping me tune the rare instrument. "In the Old Country, they knew how to make fiddles, and they knew how to make music!"

I suddenly realized I'd been hearing about this Old Country all my life and still knew almost nothing about it.

"Where was the Old Country?" I asked her. "And why did you leave it? You've never told me."

"Ah . . . ," she said softly, her face blossoming into a smile. "I've been waiting for you to ask. In the Old Country, every winter was a hundred years and every spring a miracle; in the

Old Country, the water was like music and the music was like water. It's where all the fairy tales come from, where there was magic and there was war. It's where I was a little girl and where I was a fox."

"What do you mean, you were a fox?" It was hard enough to believe she was ever a little girl. "Do you mean you were smart as a fox?"

"As smart and as stupid," she said, and looked straight into my eyes with her golden ones. "I was a fox. With a tail!"

She saw the confusion on my face and laughed. "It was in the Old Country where there were lots of foxes . . . and magic . . . long, long ago. . . ."

"Please tell me," I said.

Her eyes went a shade darker, her face serious, and this is what she told me.

1

Long ago, in an old, old country, a little girl named Gisella lived on a small farm surrounded by woods and mountains. She lived with her mother, brother, grandfather, and Great-Aunt Tanteh. They had a horse to ride and to pull the plow; a goat for milk and cheese; a sheep for wool; a pig for a pet; a cat to catch mice and purr by the fire; a rooster to crow; and lots of fat red, white, and yellow hens. And one black one. And in the spring, when the snow melted and the streams ran full, loud, and fast and the hens began laying again, it was Gisella's job to collect the eggs from the chicken house.

In the shadowy freshness of dawn, she would go out barefoot over the cold, wet grass where old mother spider's webs caught the dewdrops for her morning tea. In the chicken house, it was dim and dusty, cool and smelly, full of the mutter and murmur of the hens.

She would wish them each a good morning as she tickled them around their wattles the way Great-Aunt had taught her.

If she did it properly, she could slip her other hand under them and take out the new, warm eggs, delicate as china cups, wisps of straw still stuck to them, and put them in the big basket her mother had made.

There were twelve hens, each named for a different month of the year: January, February, Marcia, and so on.

On the first day of April, the Day of Fools, she found the hen named for that month gone, her nest empty. Gisella ran to the shed where her big brother, Tavido, was milking the goat.

"April is gone," she said.

He ran to the empty nest and sniffed the floor all around it.

"The fox!" he said as he stood up. He was tall, and his downy new whiskers glittered like gold in the morning sun. She ran after him to the house. Mother, Grandfather, and Great-Aunt Tanteh sat at the big table with steaming bowls of hot milk and chunks of black bread dripping with honey and butter. Nubia, their big calico cat, lapped his milk by the fire.

"The fox," said Tavido. "That vixen we've seen. She took April."

"Poor April," said Mother, shaking her head as Great-Aunt mumbled sounds like a broody hen. Grandfather struck the table with his fist, got up, took the long rifle down from over the door, and gave it to Tavido. Mother wrapped some bread, salty cheese, and honey cake in a bandanna and put them into Tavido's leather bag along with a handful of lead bullets. They all followed him out the door, into the yard, and he started toward the woods, when Great-Auntie said, "Listen."

They listened. They heard a clomping, regular and rhythmic. They could feel it in the earth.

"Run!" Grandfather said to Tavido. "Run to the woods." The clomping became stronger and louder with every clomp.

But the boy just stood there, looking down the road that came past their house. Now with the clomping they heard a jingling, getting louder, getting closer.

"Run, Tavido!" clucked Great-Aunt Tanteh. "Run!" Now there were drums along with the jingling and clomping.

"Run to the woods!" His mother shook him, her shout all but drowned out by the drumming and clomping and jingling.

But Gisella's brother stood like a tall blond statue, spellbound by the sound, looking down the road.

"I'm not afraid of them," he said. "I'm not afraid of anything."

Then around the bend came marching drummers all in black, beating big red drums. Behind them on a black horse rode a general in a long black coat and silver helmet studded with spear points. He had a big black mustachio that stood way out on either side of his nose, like horns. Behind him marched the soldiers, with their black rifles on their shoulders, a bayonet on each rifle.

"Halt!" shouted the general, raising his sword high above his head. With a clash and a jingle, they stopped in front of the house.

In the sudden silence, from far off, Gisella heard a fox bark.

"Young man!" The general called to her brother. "You're a Crag, aren't you?"

"Yes, sir!" shouted Tavido proudly, saluting and snapping to attention. He and his family were indeed Crags. Surland Crags, for Surland was the kingdom in which they lived. Gisella's ancestors were said to have come to Surland from some far northern craggy mountains over a thousand years before, but around the farm, they still spoke their old Craggy language and sang their old songs and told their old stories. Some people didn't like them because of that.

"Are you a coward like most of your kind?" asked the general.

"No, sir!" shouted Tavido fiercely.

"Do you love your country, Surland, and your queen, Sydnia the Sweet, may the gods bless and keep her?"

"*Sir!*" shouted the young man, staring straight ahead, his eyes blazing.

"Do you know how to use that gun?" asked the general.

"*Sir!*"

"Good boy! Fall in behind me! You're in the army!"

Tavido's mother screamed a long scream and threw her arms around his neck.

"No, no!" she wailed. "You mustn't go! I can't bear to lose you!"

"Mother . . . ," he said, pulling her arms away. "Don't worry! Grandpa, Great-Auntie, Gisella, take care of her . . . and prepare a hero's welcome for my return!" He took a place in the first rank. His mother fell to her knees and the rest of his family seemed turned to stone as the general ordered, "Forwaaard . . . *march!*"

And off went Tavido, led by the pounding drums, followed by the clomping boots, counting in cadence, "hup, two, three, four. . . ."

It seemed to take forever for the army to pass, and when it was gone, echoing off into the distance, the family stood by the road in the settling dust. On her knees, the mother wailed and wept and Gisella was crying, too. Her mother had often told her how her father, just before she was born, had gone off the same way and had never returned.

"War is coming again," crooned Great-Aunt Tanteh.

Grandpa nodded. "War again."

Just then a chicken squawked, and Gabriel, their rooster, began to crow. Turning, they saw a streak of orange and white flash between bush and tree. They ran to the henhouse. The door was open, swinging loose, and inside, Gabriel crowed and crowed, and the rattled chickens perched, clucking, around the rafters. Straw and feathers floated in the air. May was gone.

"That fox is shameless!" shouted the grandfather, shaking his fist at the forest.

"I will catch the fox," said Gisella.

They all looked at her.

"You're a girl," said her grandfather.

"You're twelve, just a baby," said her mother. "You mustn't go!"

"I'm going," she said. She was very sad and very angry.

"Just remember . . . ," muttered Great-Aunt Tanteh like an old hen, "never look too long into the eyes of a fox."

Gisella had heard her say that a million times but never really understood what she meant by it. Gisella wrapped some black bread and white cheese in her kerchief. She stood on a stool and reached down her father's crossbow and arrows, which always hung beside the door. She headed off into the woods.

"Please be careful!" called her mother.

"Good luck!" called her grandfather.

"Remember . . . ," called Great-Aunt Tanteh.

2

In the chill, dim forest, the low morning sun flashed gold and white through the leaves. Birds called, near, then far. The robin and the thrush. The cuckoo and the bobolink. Gisella's bare feet were silent on the soft moss carpeting the root-tangled path that wove between the trees into the deep woods. The smells were fresh morning forest smells, but she thought she could still catch a hint of hen and a sharp tang of fox. Here and there, like tiny white flowers, chicken feathers lay on the path. She was listening for clucks and squawks, hoping May was still alive, when something large and soft rubbed against her. She looked down to see Nubia padding alongside, his coat blending in with the browns and blacks of the woods, his eyes with the greens.

"Dear Nubia," she said, "I'm so glad you've come to keep me company. You will help me catch the fox." He looked up at her and mewed and then turned his attention back to the path.

Deeper in the woods, the trees were taller. More birdsong echoed back and forth overhead, though no birds could be seen. Great-Aunt Tanteh said that birds see everything that happens and sing about it. Gisella wondered if they were singing about Nubia and her. About the fox and May and April. She imagined they sang, "Here comes Gisella with her friend, that bird-eating cat! They don't know the fox is just ahead of her, hiding behind that bush, that shattered tree trunk, waiting, chewing on a chicken bone. Birds, keep to the air!"

Something caught her eye in a pond of brackish water beside the path. A large pale green moth had just crawled up out of the water onto a stalk of grass and was trying to dry its wings. It was unaware that, just behind it, a huge frog was poised, about to snatch it with its sticky tongue. Gisella quickly tossed a pebble into the pond, and the frog was gone. She reached down and let the moth crawl onto her finger. She gently blew the water off its translucent wings. It tried them, up and down a few times. Then it flew off among the trees.

The light poured down in glowing beams, picking out a crimson mushroom or a purple trillium, and Gisella became aware that something was moving quietly not far ahead of her.

Between the trees and bushes, she glimpsed a figure in brown and gray following the same path up and down the hillocks. She came closer and closer, but the person didn't seem to notice. He or she was cloaked and hooded, not much taller than Gisella. Then she noticed that Nubia was no longer beside her. Her heart beat faster. Great-Aunt Tanteh always told her that, when you met someone in these woods, you could never be sure if it was a person . . . or something else. One of the forest sprites or some animal in disguise. "In these woods," she had said, "things may not be what they seem. Things change; now it's this, then it's that. Look closely, be careful, and never look too long into the eyes of a fox."

Gisella followed the person for quite a while at a quick pace until she looked around and realized they were in strange woods on a path she didn't know. Now she felt a flutter of panic. Finally, right behind the stranger, she said, "Excuse me. . . ." The person seemed not to hear.

"Excuse me," she said again. The person stopped, and Gisella froze. It turned around. The person resembled an owl, with huge yellowy eyes and a small beaked nose.

"I'm looking for a fox," said Gisella. "He's been stealing our chickens."

The owl person blinked and stared at her crossbow. "What," it said, "are you going to do with that thing?"

"When I find the fox, I am going to kill it."

"You are a killer?"

"I am a hunter. The fox is the murderer. He's killing our chickens. My brother just went off to the army. My grandfather

is old; Mother has to take care of my great-aunt, who's very old.
I must hunt the fox. Have you seen it?"

"Follow your nose," said the person. "You'll find the fox.
But . . ."

Gisella waited for the rest. "But . . . what?"

"You mustn't kill her unless you're sure she's guilty. She
must have a trial."

"But I know she's guilty," said Gisella. "She took our beautiful chickens." She had heard of trials from her grandfather.
They happened in the distant capital. He read to her about them
in newspapers he sometimes brought from the village.

"Maybe she just helped them to escape," said the stranger.
"Maybe they're alive and free, content to lay eggs for themselves . . . thanks to the fox. Have a trial. Let justice prevail.
That's my advice." He walked past Gisella and disappeared
among the trees.

Her heart was thumping hard. Was it a person? Was it an
owl? She wasn't sure. She held the crossbow a little tighter.
A trial indeed! For that thieving, murdering fox! She took a
deep breath and waited a moment till the pounding in her
ears subsided.

The birds were quiet now. Her feet moved silently on the
soft forest floor. It was completely still. Then she realized
she felt something with the soles of her feet. A thumping. In
the earth. Like her heart, like the army, but different—not

rhythmic, not regular. She stopped and listened. From way off, she heard and felt it.

Boom.

Boom, boom . . . Boom! . . . nothing, and then again . . . *Boom!* Never before had she heard or felt anything like it. But somehow she knew what it was.

It was war.

3

In a grassy clearing roofed by the flickering leaves of surrounding trees, Gisella came to a fallen oak. Its roots clutched at the air like an enormous hand, the fingers all twisted and pointing in different directions. She saw a white feather near it. She tiptoed close and found, hidden under the trunk, a hole in the ground. The fox's home.

She settled down behind a patch of flowering brambles, pointed her crossbow at the hole, and waited. The light had changed. It was now dim and gray, the air damp and chill. From time to time, she felt the distant thumps. She was hungry but afraid to move. She waited. The longer she waited, the more she felt someone was watching her—someone behind her. Someone with yellow eyes. Gisella turned her head slowly and there was the fox, close enough that Gisella could see her whiskers twitch. She sat and looked directly into Gisella's eyes.

Gisella had seen many foxes. She'd met them in the woods

or running through a meadow. They'd exchange looks. But she always heard Great-Auntie saying, "Just remember . . . ," and she never looked too long. She never thought to ask what might happen if she did. Gisella thought it was one of those old superstitions that would bring bad luck, like spilling salt or breaking a mirror. And so now, again, she took her eyes from the fox's and brought her crossbow around.

Her brother had taught her how to shoot. She aimed at the fox's chest. She had never killed anything before. She wondered if she could do it now. Her anger at the theft of the chickens and sadness at the loss of her brother were gone. She was alone, aiming an arrow at a fox who looked her in the eyes.

"What about my trial?" said the fox. "And why can't you look me in the eye?"

Gisella was startled. A talking fox! She had a small, nasal voice, like a little violin. An enchanted fox, thought Gisella. Then anger replaced surprise. "You stole our chickens," she said. "Give them back!"

"But, my dear girl," said the fox, "I didn't steal them. My lawyer will prove it, although really, you're the one who should do the proving. I'm completely innocent."

"How can there be a trial?" asked Gisella. "Where's the court? Where're the judge and jury?"

"We'll be the jury!" cawed a harsh voice, and she looked up to see a large crow perched on a branch above the fox. And on branches all around, there were other birds of all kinds. "We'll be the jury!" they sang in a chorus.

"And I am the judge," said a voice like a whisper of wind, small, but every word ringing in the open space. Gisella saw a dot of light descending in the middle of the clearing. It was a pure white spider lowering itself on its thread. It stopped at about Gisella's height and hung there, seeming to float in air.

"Order in the court," it said.

Around the edge of the clearing she now saw animals of all kinds—squirrels, hedgehogs, deer, snakes and toads, a wolf, and a huge black bear—all watching her. Mixed among them were little people—some no taller than a toadstool—young and old, with pale green skin and pale green eyes, all dressed in soft shades of dark green and brown. They sat quietly and watched, but if Gisella looked directly at one, it disappeared. She sat down also and tried not to tremble.

"Lawyer for the plaintiff!" called the spider judge. Into the grassy clearing bounded Nubia, the cat. Gisella had never been so glad to see anyone. Or so surprised.

"I was sorry to have to leave you alone," he said. "I was preparing our case. Don't worry, the facts are on our side."

"But how is it you can speak? And how is it I can understand the fox and the birds, and the spider judge?"

"This clearing is a place where worlds meet. A kind of crossroads. The human world, the animal world, and the invisible world are all open to each other here, and in other places like this. Here, we all understand each other."

"And how did you get to be a lawyer?" Gisella asked him.

"Night school," he said, and sat beside her with his tail curled around him.

"Lawyer for the accused," said the judge. The owl-faced stranger waddled into the clearing, bowed to the judge, and sat near the fox. Was it a person or a very large horned owl? Gisella couldn't be sure.

"Begin with the accusations," the judge ordered.

Nubia gave his tail a lick and began to pace back and forth before the judge.

"Your honor," he said, "birds of the jury, we will easily prove that this . . . fox . . . ," and he glared and hissed at the fox, "has stolen my client's plump, juicy chickens in order to dine on them. In other words, to eat them—all—up!"

"Objection!" screeched the owl-person. "That's a lie!"

"Order," whispered the judge. "The defense may now respond."

The owl-person arranged his cloak, which seemed to be made of feathers, and paced before them.

"We will show that these chickens, unwilling captives of the accuser and her cruel family, begged my client, this honest fox, to help them escape their servitude, to live as free citizens of these woods, like all of you here."

"All lies!" hissed Nubia, lunging at the owl, who flapped its arms (or were they wings) and hissed back. They glared at each other. The owl took refuge behind the fox. Gisella glanced at the fox, and it looked right into her eyes. She looked away.

"First witness," said the judge. One of the small people that ringed the court came shyly but quickly into the center of the clearing. If Gisella looked at him from the corners of her eyes, he didn't fade away. He had pretty little features, skin and eyes the color of new leaves, and long dark green hair like pond grass.

"Say your name," said the judge, "and what you witnessed and when."

"I am called Quick," said the little person, quickly, each word a different note, like singing. "This morning before the dew was dry, I saw a fox drag a chicken into this clearing, rip it open, and devour it; she cracked its bones, sucked them dry, and ate them, too, and then licked her paws and whiskers. I saw it all. It's all I saw."

"Did this chicken," asked Nubia, "seem eager or willing to be the fox's breakfast?"

"I didn't ask," said the little person.

"Was this chicken named May, or was it named April?"

"It didn't say."

"No further questions," said Nubia. The owl waddled out from behind the fox and paced the grass.

"Was the fox you saw this fox?" it asked.

"I have no idea," said the witness. "All foxes look alike to me." And he faded away and was gone.

"Next witness," said the judge. A chicken's head looked warily out of the fox's hole, this way and that. It was April.

"April," called Gisella. "It's me, Gisella, come to take you home." The hen looked at her, and then looked away. She walked out before the judge. She appeared nervous.

"Say your name," said the spider, "and how you came to be here."

"April, your worship," she clucked and muttered. "In the early dark of dawn, I was awakened by a voice whispering in the hen dialect, 'I'm here to free you so your eggs will not be eaten and you can have chicks that are free, and their chicks, and their chicks' chicks will be free.' I asked this voice, 'What is "free"?' and it answered, 'Free is what every creature longs to be and has a right to be.' Then something took me firmly but gently by the neck and carried me out of the chicken house, just as the others were waking. It was the fox. I'd always heard horrible stories about foxes—what they do to chickens—but I wasn't afraid. I don't know why not. It brought me here and hid me in its hole." April began to cluck and anxiously turn in circles. "I don't like talking like this, answering questions. I'm just a poor hen!" She was becoming more and more upset. The owl-person waddled up to her and tried to calm her.

"Now, now, we know it's been an ordeal. We appreciate what you've been through. We're here to help. Just one more question, one more, that's all. Did this fox harm or hurt you in any way?"

"No, no she didn't."

"No further questions," said the owl, and stepped back. Nubia took her turn.

"Were you ever mistreated by this girl, Gisella, or any member of her family? Didn't they always feed you and house you and care for you?"

"Yes! Yes!" screeched the hen. "But they took my eggs! Every day I laid, and she came and took my eggs! And then, when one of us became old, or injured, one of her family would come and wring our neck! What do I know? I'm only a chicken! They feed us and they keep us stupid! And you!" She charged at Nubia, quite carried away. "You've looked at me and licked your dripping chops, your little white pointed teeth! You'd make a meal of me if you could . . . and YOU, TOO!" Now she turned on the owl-person. "You're the same! Acting so wise—you'd like to get your claws into my flesh! Don't deny it! I see it in your yellow eyes! They've all got yellow eyes! I'm a poor hen and the world only sees me as dinner!" She had become completely hysterical and ran circles all over the clearing, and it was clear that she was right. Nubia as well as the owl and the fox followed her with their yellow eyes, and they all looked ready to spring.

"Order," said the spider judge, and April ran, madly clucking, back into the fox's hole. The lawyers and the defendant all stared after her.

"Next witness," said the judge.

"Where is May?" asked Gisella. "Where is my other hen? She should be a witness, too!"

"She is," said the judge. "Will the hen called May please step forward?"

"I can't," said a muffled voice. It came from the fox, who belched and then looked all around, as if to see where the voice and belch had come from.

"I'm May," said the voice from the fox, whose mouth never moved. She looked up at the trees like a ventriloquist misdirecting the audience. "But I'm barely May," the voice continued. "Little by little, I feel myself becoming fox. A part of me is becoming her liver. Another part is becoming her tongue; I'm even becoming her teeth. It's a very odd sensation."

"Does it hurt, May?" Gisella called to her.

"Not really, not now," she answered. "It hurt when she woke me in the chill before dawn. She dragged me away into the blackness of the woods, to this place. And here, she devoured me."

"Would you say," asked Nubia, "that she ate you all up?"

"I would," said May. "It was strangely calming, for I felt no pain. As it was happening, I suddenly remembered hatching from an egg. And this was like being stuffed back into an egg. Like being born in reverse. And now . . . I'm becoming . . . fox. Good-bye . . . good-bye . . ." The voice became less and less distinct and faded away.

"Good-bye, May," Gisella sobbed. "Good-bye." May had been her favorite hen. "You are a murderer!" Gisella screamed at the fox. "A thief and a murderer!"

"Order in this court," whispered the spider. "Fox, do you have a name?"

"My name," said the fox, "is Flame."

"How do you answer the charges against you?"

"I am a fox," said the fox. Gisella waited for more. There was silence.

"Is that your defense?" asked the spider.

"Yes," said the fox. "I am a fox. I live by my nose, by my teeth and feet. By my wits. How can I steal? How can one creature own another—except to eat it? Don't we all belong to ourselves? Until someone else—someone bigger, faster, hungrier, smarter—catches us? And eats us? I didn't steal. I hunted. I didn't murder. I fed. I am accused of being a fox. If that's a crime, then so is being an owl, or a cat . . . or a spider. Or a girl." She looked at Gisella. Everyone looked at her.

Boom . . . boom, boom . . . She felt it in the earth.

"Do you, the plaintiff, Gisella, have anything to say?" the judge asked her.

She stood up. "I believe the fox. We each do what we must to live. I love our chickens and do my best to protect them. She loves them in her way, and does her best to catch them. The jury will decide if these are crimes. But if I catch her taking our chickens again, I will kill her. I give her fair warning. And if that's a crime, do to me what you must."

The birds of the jury chattered and squawked for a long time while Gisella waited. They rattled and ruffled their feathers. Then they became quiet. The large crow coughed and cleared his throat.

"Jury," said the spider, "have you reached a verdict?"

"We have a verdict, your honor," said the crow.

"How do you find the defendant: guilty or not guilty?"

"We find the defendant, Flame—the fox whom we hate and fear because she kills and devours birds and small animals—we find her to be innocent."

"Court dismissed," said the spider. "It's time for my tea." She rode quickly up her thread like a sunbeam, and in that instant, everyone else was gone. The clearing was still and empty, except for the fox, and Nubia and Gisella. She looked at the fox and the fox looked at her. They looked into each other's eyes, and this time, Gisella did not look away.

4

Gisella looked into the fox's yellow eyes to show her she wasn't afraid and that she would stand up for what was hers. She also looked to see what she would find there, to discover what it was her great-aunt had warned her against.

The fox's eyes were dark gold. They looked at her with calm curiosity, to see what she would do. They challenged her to look deeper. They were the color of flame and they flickered. She looked deeper and saw a golden meadow under golden clouds and she saw a yellow-gold rabbit running for its life. She smelled its joy at being a rabbit and its terror at being pursued, and it seemed she was right behind it, running like the wind. She could almost taste it and thought she almost had it, when she heard laughter. She blinked and she was back in the grassy clearing. It was as if she'd wakened from a dream. In front of her stood a girl of about her age. The girl had a red kerchief and long black braids like Gisella's. Her blue flowered skirt was like Gisella's also, and she held a crossbow.

"So this is what it's like to have fingers," the girl laughed, and pointed the bow at Gisella. "How does the world look from the other side of the crossbow?"

Gisella knew this girl. She was so very familiar that it took a moment to realize who she was. Gisella was looking at herself. She looked down. The grass was suddenly close, and instead of hands, she had two little black fox feet. Behind her she found a long, white-tipped fox tail. The fox had changed places with her. This was what Great-Aunt Tanteh had warned her of. While Gisella looked into her eyes, the fox had slipped into Gisella's body, and now Gisella was in the fox's.

Now I am a fox, she thought, and the fox is me.

"Give me back my body!" she barked. But the fox only laughed. Gisella saw a brown-faced, barefoot girl laughing and pointing at her. The fox-girl twirled on Gisella's toes, and Gisella's long blue skirt flared. Gisella's braids flew around her.

"Oh, no!" she said. "It's not often a fox finds someone foolish enough to look long enough, deep enough into its eyes. I'll keep your body till I'm good and ready to give it back. Meanwhile, you'll find that being a fox can be lots of fun. Mind you take care of my coat and groom my tail! Come, Nubia, let's go home and see to the chickens."

"Don't worry about the trial Gisella," said Nubia. "We'll appeal to a higher court. I'll prepare arguments and gather petitions; it's not over yet!" He strolled to the fox-girl, rubbed against her legs, and purred. "Good-bye for now," he said to Gisella. "And good luck in your new life."

"Nubia!" she cried. "How can you leave me here all alone in the woods?"

"We must all play the roles we are given, Gisella," he said. "Yours is being a fox. This is where you live. My role is finding some way to help you while I lap milk and purr by the fire."

"Nubia! I'm coming home with you!"

Flame the fox-girl aimed the crossbow at Gisella. "Stay away from my house, fox!" she said. "And stay away from my chickens! If you come near them, I will shoot you! I give you fair warning. Do those words sound familiar?" An arrow whistled past Gisella's ear. She leapt behind the fallen tree and the fox-girl laughed again.

"Yes," called Flame as she left the clearing, "I think you'll enjoy being a fox!" And with Nubia right beside her, tail held high, she disappeared, laughing, into the woods.

"Good-bye," called Nubia. "Good luck!"

Gisella sat down and began to cry. The tears ran down her long muzzle and dripped off her nose, onto her paws. After a long while, she heard someone muttering and clucking. It was April, sticking her head up out of the fox's hole.

"Is that awful trial business over?" she asked. "It made me so nervous, all those questions, all those eyes. . . ." She shuddered and ruffled her feathers.

"April," Gisella said, "don't you know me? I'm Gisella. The fox changed places with me and went home with Nubia."

"Please!" screeched April. "Don't say things like that. It makes me dizzy! Gisella is Gisella, you are a fox, and I am a chicken. I am a hungry chicken. Where is the corn you promised me? Where is the millet of freedom? Where is Great-Aunt Tanteh holding up the corners of her apron full of crumbs?"

"That is all at home," said Gisella. "I will take you back, April, I promise, but if they see me looking like this, they will kill me." She looked around the darkening clearing. "I think I know the way. . . ." She sniffed the late-afternoon air and was startled at all she found there: birds nestling into their nests, badgers crawling into their holes, bees settling into their hives— a new world of countless surprising smells, but none of them said "home." The colors of the woods were fading to gray. Far to the west, like dying coals on the hearth, she saw glimpses of an orange-and-red sunset through the trees. An overwhelming tiredness filled her body.

"It will be dark soon," she said. "We must wait till morning."

"Yes . . . ," yawned April. "I am a hungry chicken, but I am also a sleepy chicken. The darker, the sleepier. It's time to settle, it's time to roost, to disappear into my nice new nest." She hopped back into the fox's hole. Gisella stuck her nose in and sniffed. It smelled strongly of fox, but she didn't mind. She crawled in and found a low-ceilinged room with no corners. The ceiling became the walls, and the walls became the floor, and all were made of dirt veined with tree roots. April was already settled cozily against the wall. Curled up against her, Gisella licked the salt of her tears off her nose and whiskers.

Last night, she thought, I slept under a goose-feather comforter in a snug house with my family snoring all around me. Tonight, I sleep in the body of a fox in a fox's hole with a chicken. What will tomorrow bring? She fell asleep.

5

She dreamed she was in her mother's arms, being gently rocked and hummed a lullaby. She could feel her mother's heart beating strong against her. *Boom, boom, boom.* Half-awake in the night, she realized it was the pounding she felt—*Boom! Boom!*—in the earth all around her. Maybe it's the earth's heart beating, she thought. Maybe it's thunder. Maybe it will rain and, cozy in my hole, I'll hear the pattering on the leaves above me. Her eyelids flickered and she saw a flash of white light. Lightning, she thought.

She felt another *boom,* and slept again. The deepest sleep she'd ever known. She slept on and on and dreamt of carnivals and fireworks and storms raging on and on. . . .

"Gisehh-laaaa! Gisehh-laaaa!"

She heard a voice singing her name. She yawned, opened her eyes, and blinked. It took a minute before she remembered where she was. And what she was. Slowly she inched her nose out of the hole. She saw the dark blue light of just before dawn.

"Gisehh-laaaa," sang the voice again. A luminous green moth fluttered just over her head. It landed on the fallen tree above the hole and became Quick, the small forest person she'd seen in the trial. He glowed with a soft green light. With her fox eyes she could look directly at him and he didn't disappear.

"Gisella," he said, "we must go now."

"How long have I been sleeping?" she asked.

He shrugged. "A day or two or three or four," he said.

"How could I have slept so long?" she cried. "I must get back into my own body!"

"Do you remember the moth you saved from a frog?" Quick asked. Gisella had to think a moment before she nodded. "I was that moth," he said. "Because you helped me, I will help you. While you slept, the war has begun. One army fought another right here. The cannons roared and blasted. Look what they've done to these woods! Our beautiful woods!"

Gisella looked out. The clearing was all mud. It was torn and cratered. Trees were shattered, some fallen and others blown to splinters. The ground was littered with broken branches. She smelled burnt and dead things, and a strange bitter odor that seemed to come from everywhere. She tried to imagine what might have caused such awful destruction and trembled. Her fox belly felt icy.

"Now the defeated army is returning," said Quick, "with

more soldiers and guns and horrible things that I don't understand. Listen!" She heard the approaching marchers tramping and a low grumbling rumble that made her fur rise.

"This battle will be even worse. My people are leaving. We are going to the end of the invisible world, to the far invisible mountains where it's safe. You and your friend must come with us. Come now, come quickly!"

"What about my mother?" said Gisella, "and my grandfather and Great-Aunt Tanteh? I must go and see what's become of them! And most of all, I have to get back into my own body!"

"No time! No time!" said Quick. "You're much better off as a fox. Foxes don't need big ugly houses and all those things humans have! Pots and pans and chairs and pictures and doors and wagons and fences and spoons—how do you keep track of it all? Then you fight over it! Isn't that why you have wars? Then you blow it all to bits! What's the sense of it?"

"I will not be a fox!" cried Gisella. "That thief called Flame steals my chickens, gets off free, and then steals my body! She won't get away with it! I'll . . . I'll . . . try her again or whatever it takes—but I must get my own body back! Please help me!" Quick stared at her. Then he jumped up and hopped in circles, waving his arms.

"Don't you understand?" he pleaded. "There's no time for a trial and your lawyer was terrible! Flame the fox has longed all her life for fingers and chickens. She's not going to just give them up. You'd have to trick her into it, and do you know how hard it is to fool a fox? Have you any idea? We must go now! *Now!* First, you want to get your body, then you'll want something else! I know you people! You're so slow! You'll want to stop for breakfast, then for lunch, then to rest! Helping you is so difficult! I don't know if I can do it!" He leapt into the air and became a ruby-throated hummingbird. He zoomed all around the clearing and landed back on the tree as himself.

"All right!" he said, shaking his long green hair. "You saved my life. I'll take you to your family. I'll help you as best I can— but hurry!"

"I will," said Gisella. "I promise!" She called into the hole, "April! Wake up! It's time to go!"

"It isn't," muttered April's voice. "There's been no cock-a-doodle-doo."

"Gabriel's not here," said Gisella. "We're in the woods. The war is coming!" She heard the army's tramping and rumbling, closer now. "Quick's right. We must go now!"

"I don't do anything," clucked April, "nothing—till I hear a cock-a-doodle-do!"

Gisella looked at Quick. He was hopping in circles again and pulling his hair. "You people!" he cried. "You people!" Then he jumped onto the fallen tree, threw back his hair, and crowed.

"Cock-a-doodle-doooo!"

April's head popped out of the hole. "I'm ready," she said, and flapped her way out. Gisella looked at her and grew dizzy. Her belly was empty. April looked and smelled like a warm, succulent, feathered pie. Gisella's mouth fell open and her jaws dripped.

"I'm so hungry," she said. "I need to eat a little something before we go."

"I knew it, I knew it!" fumed Quick.

"Dear April," said Gisella, "would you lay me an egg, please—or two? Please."

"So! I'm just an egg factory to you, too! Freedom indeed! Freedom to feed foxes!"

"I beg you," said Gisella. "I'm so hungry. Please . . ."

"Very well. Why not? Why not! Tickle my wattles."

"Eggs! Wattles!" Quick gnashed his teeth and then fluttered overhead as a moth. With her long nose under April's beak, Gisella tickled her wattles as best she could. It was all she could do not to take a bite out of her. The tramping in the ground was now coming from at least two directions. There was more than one army. And the strange rumbling had become a frightening low, pulsing roar.

"How can I do it with all this racket!" wailed April. "I need peacefulness!" April clucked, Gisella tickled, and soon there was an egg. Gisella cracked it with her teeth, swallowed down the warm, sweet yolk, and licked the shell. She'd never eaten anything better.

"Thank you, dear April," she said. "You saved my life!" And maybe, thought Gisella, her own as well. She couldn't swear she wouldn't have eaten her dear chicken friend.

"Off we go," said Quick, dropping down in front of them. "April, ride on Gisella's back; I'll lead the way. Hurry!" He became a hummingbird again and sped ahead into the woods. With April on her back, Gisella sped after him.

Flame was right about one thing: Being a fox could be fun! Running in the fox's body, Gisella felt like an arrow shot from a bow. The ground blurred beneath her, and trees seemed to jump out of the way. She rushed through a sea of smells that sang of everything around her—the plants, the trees, the mushrooms, all the animals and birds, and even worms in the ground.

Her tongue fluttered in the wind and she tasted the sunlit air. She felt as wild as the woods felt she could run around the world without ever stopping.

But under everything were the smells of leather and sweat, metal and things she didn't yet know the names of, oily smells that burned her nostrils. She kept her eye on Quick, and after a while, the woods became familiar and some of the smells, too: goat and pig, the chicken house, the cinnamon scent of her mother, Grandfather's pipe, and Great-Aunt Tanteh's snuff. They were close to home! She ran faster. And then she

remembered and slowed. They wouldn't see her, Gisella, but a
fox who had stolen their chickens. And the real fox was there
now. With them. Sitting around the table with bowls of warm
milk, with black bread dripping with honey and butter. . . . The
fox was with them in her body!

"We're there! Were here!" clucked April, flapping her wings.
"We're home!"

They had come to the edge of the field behind the house.
Gisella stopped and sniffed. In the mix of smells, she smelled a
cold hearth and felt a chill.

"Hurray!" cried April. "Hurry to the corn, to the crumbs!
Hurray!"

"You go ahead," Gisella said to her. April hopped off
Gisella's back and ran muttering happily into the field. Gisella
heard the sound of her feathers brushing through the tall
spring grass and realized how very quiet it had suddenly
become. She lowered her body and cautiously, silently followed, listening for voices, the bleat of the goat, the grunt of
the pig, the clucking chickens, her mother's singing. She heard
nothing but the beating of her own heart. When she came to
the house and her great-aunt's garden, she stopped. The sweet,
lingering scents of everyone she loved hung like ghosts in the
air. But she saw no one.

The pigsty was empty. April clucked and pecked around the

deserted chicken house. Its door gaped open. The door to the house was open, too.

Gisella ran inside and trotted frantically from room to empty room. Nothing was left. Clothes, pots, dishes, bowls, spoons, the butter churn, the spinning wheel, pictures, her father's old fiddle, the feather beds, even her doll, Gretel—everything was gone. She caught the scent of each object fading. The scent of each person disappearing. First she'd lost her brother. Her body was no longer hers. And now, the rest of her family had vanished.

6

A great explosion knocked her off her little black feet and sent her tumbling into a corner. Blast after blast of cannons and the rifles' crack and boom made a sudden wall of sound through which she heard hundreds of soldiers shouting and running. She peeked around the edge of the open door. The air was full of smoke. The general who had taken her brother galloped through the troops, waving his sword and shouting curses. The soldiers' faces were smeared with dirt. Some dragged a leg or supported a comrade. Their uniforms were torn and many were bloody. Horses pulled a clattering wagon full of wounded and she heard their groans and cries over the explosions that thudded closer and closer. She tried to see every face, searching for her brother, but there were too many. There was a long, piercing whistle, louder and louder, and the ground across the road erupted with a blast that sent a geyser of fire, earth, and smoke high into the sky and knocked her sprawling again. The soldiers began to run faster. Another whistle, another blast, and then another and another, so loud and close she thought for sure she'd be blown to bits. The windows shattered. Earth, rocks, and tree branches battered the roof like a monstrous hailstorm. Her fur stood on end. With her tail wrapped around her, trembling and panting in terror, she flattened herself to the floor.

Through the broken window, she saw uprooted oaks and tumbling boulders hang in the dirty sky before falling back to earth. Then she realized the rumbling roar she'd heard before was loud and full now. Now a different army, all in purple, was running past. Their general rode a two-wheeled metal horse. He shouted in a language that sounded like coughing and choking. And then, with clanking and grinding, she saw huge windowless metal wagons with long guns sticking out in all directions. They had no horses or wheels but seemed to crawl on their armored bellies. They roared and their guns boomed and their stink seared her nostrils and lungs. They rumbled past and fired at the fleeing soldiers of the first army. The monstrous vehicles kept passing till there was a blast so close and deafening, she heard only a great bubble of silence. The roof flew apart and then fell on her.

Sneezing and coughing from the dust and surprised to be alive, she crawled and wormed her way up through rafters and shingles, out into the air. Nothing moved but the smoke and settling dust. The thump of cannons was distant again. The armored wagons were gone, but the thought of them made her tremble.

She found herself in a world she didn't know. The walls of the house still stood, but the windows were blown out and the roof was all over the floor. The thick green woods across the road had become a wasteland of uprooted stumps and smoking craters, some as deep as a horse is tall. Columns of filthy smoke rose all around the horizon, turning the pale sky slowly black. Air that had been full of springtime now had a new odor, bitter and jagged. It was the smell of pain, and it was everywhere.

Gisella felt numb and completely alone. She was beyond tears.

"April!" she barked in a kind of whisper, afraid to make any noise. "Quick! Where are you?" She hadn't seen them since the bombardment began.

"April!" she called aloud. "Quick!"

She heard a weak clucking. From under the wreckage of the chicken house, April pushed her way out. Half her feathers were gone, and the rest stood out in all directions. Dazed, she staggered toward Gisella.

"April, poor thing!" Gisella cried.

"The sky is falling! The sky is falling!" April muttered. "We must tell the queen!"

She came up to Gisella and sat suddenly and heavily. Gisella licked her feathers and also the places where she had none. "Poor, dear April," crooned Gisella.

"Yes," April said. "The queen must hear of this! The sky is falling and it's not safe! Eggs might be broken! And—"

She was interrupted by a sound so unexpected and familiar, Gisella didn't know at first what it was.

"Meeoww."

Strolling through the blasted field came Nubia, tail held high.

7

  "Nubia!" called Gisella, running to meet him. "Where is everyone? Mother, Grandpa, Great-Aunt Tanteh—are they all right?" He jumped back, arched, and hissed. Then he peered at Gisella.

"Gisella?" he said, still backing up. "Is it really you?"

"Yes! Nubia! It's me!"

"You look, smell, and sound like any fox. In fact, you are a fox. How can I be sure you're not some other fox trying to trick me? What makes you Gisella?"

"Nubia, I've know you since before your eyes were open. I knew all your brothers and sisters!"

"What were their names?"

"There was Shtrudelnoodle, then Creamylappylou, Patty-squashbuckle, and the little one . . . Max."

"Gisella!" he purred. "It is you!" He came up to her and they touched noses. "It's amazing how you can be who you are even without your proper body! How could I be me without my own whiskers? Without my own tail? And yet here you are; you're a fox, but you're still Gisella. It's a mystery." Then he rubbed against her and rolled over in the dust of the road. They sat beside April while Nubia licked Gisella's fur and she licked his. Then, together, they both licked April, who still needed calming.

"Gisella," said Nubia, "I'm so sorry I lost your case, and the truth is, I have no idea how to make an appeal. I missed that class. After the trial I was so ashamed I couldn't face you, and so I lied and went off with Flame. If she had been found guilty, everything would be different now. It was my first case, Gisella. Maybe I'm not meant to be a lawyer."

"I don't know about lawyers or trials or appeals," said Gisella. "Just tell me about my family. What's become of them? Please tell me they're alive and well!"

"Yes, Gisella, they are alive—at least they were when I last saw them. Ah, so much has happened! I'll tell you every-thing.

"When the fox and I return home," he began, "everyone thinks she's you. 'I've killed the fox!' she lies. 'I shot an arrow through its heart, poor thing,' she says. 'It won't bother our chickens anymore!' And everyone is fooled and believes her. They hug and kiss her as if she's really you. I don't say any-thing. I sit by the fire. I lap my milk and listen. She gobbles up a big supper of eggs and cheese, bread and butter and asks for more.

" 'You've returned just in time,' Grandpa says. 'The war is close and will be here any minute. We must pack everything and go to the south where it's safe.' And so they wrap up big bundles of things in blankets and pile them high in the wagon with tables, beds, and upside-down chairs. The goat, pig, and sheep are tied behind, and Great-Aunt Tanteh sits on top with baskets of chickens. The horse strains to get rolling while I sit on his back and encourage him and Grandpa leads the way. Your weeping mother walks backward, looking at the house till it's hidden by the bend in the road. Flame the fox-girl walks beside her, holding her hand. There are thumping and booming noises, constant and close, and the horse stumbles from time to time.

"We roll over strange roads, past woods and fields we don't know. We see not a soul. The scattered houses are empty and still as if everyone left long before. Going up a hill between two fields, we come around a bend and see a big black boulder in the road. We approach slowly. The boulder moves and turns. It's a huge black bear. It stares, then ambles slowly toward us. Grandpa looks around for the crossbow. It's out of reach on top of the wagon. Your mother holds the fox-girl to her, and Great-Aunt clucks and worries with the chickens. The horse shies, eyes rolling. The bear strolls all around the wagon, calm as you please, sniffing the air, and then stops in front of Flame. Your mother holds her close, and Grandpa stands in front of them, stamps his feet, and shouts, 'Go Away! Get! Go on!'

"The bear ignores him and speaks to Flame. I know just a few words of the bear language—most of them naughty—unlike foxes, who know all tongues. The bear says something like, 'I'd know you anywhere, Flame, whatever form you took. Now you're not so fast. Now I can take your head in my jaws!'

"Flame peeks around your mother, crosses her eyes, and sticks out her tongue at the bear. 'Bears are stupid, Grandpa,' she says, 'and they're cowards. Poke him in the nose and watch him run!' Grandpa brings a piece of cheese from his pocket and holds it out in a trembling hand. The bear snuffles it and, still looking at Flame, snaps it up with his teeth and long black tongue. We hear a racketing-buzzing sound from the sky. We look up. Something that looks like an enormous dragonfly comes out of the clouds. The bear roars and gallops off into the fields, heading for the woods. I wisely take cover under the wagon.

"'I think it's something called an aeroplane!' gasps Grandpa. 'I've heard of them, but I didn't really believe in them!'

"'Coward! Bunny rabbit! Clown!' Flame jeers after the bear. Also, something worse in bear I won't repeat. The bear turns, snarls, and starts back toward us. Now he's really mad. But the dragonfly-thing zooms over him and the bear falls in the tall grass. The dragonfly roars in triumph and corkscrews through the air. We're huddled beneath a tree and hope it can't see us.

We watch in amazement and terror till it flies off and disappears into the sun.

"'Aeroplanes!' says Grandpa. 'I thought I knew war, but not like this.'

"Everyone is shaken and cries and hugs and pats one another, though Flame seems a bit unsure just how to behave. She looks at the others and does her best to be like them. I notice Great-Aunt Tanteh watching her from the corners of her eyes. We sit under the tree and eat something. No one talks. Grandpa's hands shake as he lights his pipe. We continue on.

"When night falls, we camp by a stream alongside the road. We make no fire. Grandpa doesn't want us to be seen. To lift our spirits, he takes up his fiddle and plays softly. From the first note, Flame stares at him and listens. She begs him for another tune and then another. Finally, he says, 'Enough. We must sleep.'

"I keep watch all night. I hear cannons and see flashes around the horizon. I know that Flame is awake also. Lying in her blanket. Listening. In the deepest part of the night, she rises without a sound and takes Grandpa's fiddle. She squats in the dark and holds it and sniffs it, stares at it and caresses it with her fingers. Just before dawn, she puts it back and returns to her blanket. Gabriel crows, and we continue south. The road is dusty. The sun is hot. We see almost no one all day, and we hear no cannons. Great-Aunt sits atop the wagon and scans the sky, watching and listening, muttering and clucking.

"'No birds,' she says, over and over. 'No birds . . .' And it's true. We haven't seen or heard a bird in days.

"That afternoon, as the shadows lengthen, we meet a man with a wagon full of sticks.

"'Where are you from and where are you heading?' he asks. He's very fat and he sweats and wheezes.

"'We're from north Surland, heading south away from the war,' says Grandpa. 'Has the enemy been here? Have you seen their soldiers? Have you seen their aeroplanes that roar through the sky?'

"'Here?' says the man, and he laughs and lights his pipe. 'Here the war is over. Norland has taken over this part of Surland. The emperor's troops are in charge.'

"'They are?' says Grandpa, his eyes wide with panic. 'But . . . but . . .'

"'Don't worry.' The man smiles and claps Grandpa on the shoulder. 'We'll all be better off. Believe me! Where are you stopping tonight?'

"Grandpa shrugs. 'Along the road,' he says. 'Near a stream. It's been a long, dusty day.'

"'Come to my place,' says the man. 'I've plenty of room and lots of food. My wife and I will make you welcome.'

"'We couldn't impose on you, sir,' says Grandpa.

"'Nonsense,' says the man. 'I see you have a fiddle. You can entertain us. We love a bit of music.'

"'So do I!' cries Flame excitedly.

"'Is this your daughter?' asks the man.

"'My granddaughter. She's developed a sudden passion for the fiddle.'

"'Then it's settled,' says the man. 'You'll come and stay the night.'

"'Only if we can pay you. We have money. . . .'

"'No, no!' says the man. 'Hospitality is its own reward. Come! We're just down this road. Follow me!' It has become twilight, and the clouds are purple and pink as we rattle down a rutted road into the woods. Not a bird sings. Where have the birds gone? I wonder.

"His house is large and dark and dirty and full of heavy furniture. The man's wife is thin, with a black kerchief. She has a nervous kind of chuckle. She scuttles about the kitchen and doesn't meet anyone's eye. Your mother puts the last of the cheese and sausage on the table. Our hostess serves up bowls of thin porridge and sour milk. The fat man slurps and wheezes and laughs. He asks questions about where we come from and what we did there, what we saw of the war, and what we left behind. Your mother speaks of Tavido and weeps.

"After dinner, if one would call it dinner, Grandpa fiddles and Flame is ecstatic till our host says, 'Beautiful, thank you, thank you, but you must be tired. Come, let me show you to your beds.'

"With his lantern he leads us into the barn where he keeps his horse. 'There's plenty of hay for beds. Please help yourselves and have a good night.' The barn is filthy and full of cobwebs. The hay is rotten. The horse blinks sadly at us, as if to say, 'See what I put up with?' Everyone makes their beds, though Grandpa grumbles, 'We'd be better off beside the road.' I climb into the rafters to keep watch.

"I must have dozed. The barn door bursts open and someone is shouting in a language that sounds like choking and coughing. A general in high black boots stands in the doorway, silhouetted against the first light. He waves a sword and stamps his boots. Everyone jumps up, trembling, from the hay, and the general waves them outside. Dazed, they stumble into the yard. I look out the loft window.

"The barn is ringed with soldiers in purple uniforms. They all have rifles with bayonets pointing at our family as they stagger out into the damp, chill dawn.

"'That's them!' cries the fat man. 'You can't trust their kind! Talking against the emperor! Full of secrets! Planting bombs! They're all spies! And look!' He points at our wagon. 'In the dead of night they loaded their wagon with my furniture, livestock, and chickens . . . they even took my fiddle! They're all thieves, their kind.'

"The family huddles in the middle of the yard. The general marches around them, glaring through a tiny lens he has clenched in his eye. He twirls his red mustachios.

"'Sir, the man's lying,' Grandpa begins. 'We're not spies—'

"'Silence!' cries the general. 'Spies! You will all be shot!' Your mother falls on her knees, weeping. But Flame steps forward and says, 'We are innocent. The fiddle is ours. We can easily prove it at the trial.'

"The general turns and stares at her. In an unexpectedly funny, squeaky little voice, he mimics, 'Prove it at the trial, prove it at the trial.' Several of the soldiers giggle.

"I think, Here's a chance to redeem my legal career, and I'm about to leap out to offer my services as lawyer for the defense, but the general leans over nose-to-nose with Flame and says, 'We don't try spies! We execute them! But you'—and he lifts her in the air by her braids—'you I will save to polish my boots!' He tosses her to the side, where soldiers surround her. He belches out orders and shovels are tossed to your mother and Grandpa and he motions them to dig. While Great-Aunt Tanteh sits on the ground rocking and muttering, they dig their graves and one for her, too. When the graves are deep, Grandpa and Mother, sobbing and wailing, stand in theirs. The general orders Great-Aunt to climb into hers, also.

"Great-Aunt gets slowly to her feet. She stands clucking for a moment. From under her shawl she slowly brings out the shiny black hen called December. It clucks and she clucks. She tickles its wattles, and the general coughs an order and points at her grave. The soldiers raise their rifles. Great-Aunt's hand comes out from under December, holding something that catches the first rays of the rising sun. The thing glows. The general, the soldiers, your mother, and Grandpa—even the fat man and his scrawny wife—all gasp.

"In Great-Aunt's hand is a golden egg."

INTERLUDE

"Great-Granny," I said, interrupting the story, and then searching for the words to best ask what I really wasn't sure I should ask. "Is all this . . . true?"

The old woman looked at me. "This is what Nubia said," she answered. She was not smiling.

"But . . . can I believe it?"

"I don't think Nubia was lying," she said.

"I mean . . . all of it?"

"It's hard to believe, isn't it?" said Great-Granny Gisella, nodding.

"I'm sorry, Great-Granny," I said, a bit ashamed of doubting. "Please! Go on!"

She looked at me for a moment, as if deciding whether to go on.

"Please. What happened next?"

"All right, this is what happened," said Great-Granny finally. "This is what Nubia said. . . ."

8

⅋ "The general's lens drops from his eye to the ground," said Nubia, "and his boot blindly crushes it as he steps forward and takes the egg from Great-Aunt's hand. He peers closely at it and weighs it in his palm.

"'Where did you get this?' he asks her.

Toothlessly, she sings to him:

> *'Remember December*
> *My black hen*
> *Lays eggs of gold*
> *But who knows when?*
> *Who knows how*
> *And who knows why?*
> *Everyone is going to die. . . .'*

"Great-Aunt Tanteh shuffles toward her grave, and the general shouts, 'Stop!' He says something to a soldier, who fetches a black iron skillet. The general cracks the egg into the skillet. There's a clunk of metal to metal, and there in a pool of mercury floats a solid gold yolk. The shell, too, is of the finest gold. The general stares at all this and mumbles to himself for a while. Then he sputters out a stream of orders and Grandpa and your mother and Great-Aunt are pulled up from their graves. A metal wagon, roaring and banging, stinky smoke pouring out the back, rattles up and everyone is loaded in.

"Flame leans from the window and cries, 'Give us back our fiddle!' At the general's order, she's given the fiddle.

"'To the emperor!' the general shouts.

"They all rattle and clatter off and I decide to come back here, to the house, to see what's become of things. I arrive just in time for the battle. I think to myself, it's the end of the world, and I dive down a deep badger hole. At the bottom, what do you think? A snarling badger.

"I'm dead, I think. But the bombs begin and we huddle together, shivering, frothing at the mouth till all is quiet. And here I am, and here you are. And I am very glad of that."

When Nubia finished his story, he licked his paws, and Gisella wept to think of her mother and grandpa digging their own graves. Nubia licked the tears that ran down her face.

"I had no idea December could lay golden eggs," she said to Nubia. "Great-Aunt Tanteh knows everything. She knows the secrets of chickens."

"Indeed she does," said April, "and I hope someday she'll tell me what they are."

"We have to find her—and Mother and Grandpa, and I must get my body back. They won't know me or love me if I'm a fox."

They heard a whirring hum and saw a flash of gold-green and scarlet. A hummingbird hovered over them. It descended to the top of April's head and became Quick, no more than two inches high.

9

  "Quick!" cried Gisella. "I'm so glad to see you, so glad you're all right!"

"All right?" said Quick. He balanced atop April's red comb. His green looked paler, and he was trembling. "Am I all right? Is anything all right? Oh, you people!" He rolled his eyes and took a deep breath to calm himself.

"When the battle began," he said, "I did what any sensible sprite would do; I took shelter in the invisible world because the invisible world was always safe. But the first blast blew me back into this world, which exploded, and back I went into the invisible one—back and forth—forth and back. . . . The noise! The stink! The war is destroying everything—this world, the invisible one, and the crossroads between them—magic is being lost—leaking away—their machines burn it up along with the stuff that makes them go. Magic is what I live on! Is anywhere safe? My head ached and I became so dizzy and so confused I found myself in Norland. That's where your family is."

"In Norland?" Gisella cried. "Are they all right?"

"I don't know," sighed Quick. "I know where they are, but not exactly where because the birds are gone. The birds used to tell me everything because they saw everything and knew everything. But they've all flown from the war. They are riding the high winds in fair skies over warm oceans of dolphins and whales; they are on their way to forests with leaves like green elephant ears and huge red flowers where mango and papaya ripen. . . . We could go there too, Gisella! We might be safe there, living with my people in the distant invisible mountains."

"Quick!" begged Gisella. "I must find my family. Now! Please!"

He covered his tiny green face with his hands and was still for a moment. Then he looked up and nodded grimly with pale jade eyes.

"Of course, you must find them," he said. "And I must help you. They are imprisoned somewhere in the capital city of Norland—maybe in a great pen where thousands of people are kept like cattle, or maybe in one of a hundred dungeons beneath the palace of the emperor Ignatz the XI, known as 'The Powerful' because of his remarkable odor. He calls himself Emperor of Norland, Weyland, Eyeland, and Inner Myopia. He wants to conquer Surland; he wants to rule the world. If he catches us, I can become a moth or a bird and have a chance of escape—a chance!—the rest of you will surely die . . . if we're not blown to bits on the way. Follow me!" And again, he was a ruby-throated hummingbird and off like a shot.

"April," Gisella barked, "jump onto my back! Come Nubia, follow Quick! We mustn't lose him!"

And skirting craters and leaping fallen trees, after him they went, as fast as they could go. Every now and again, Quick, with a flash of green and scarlet, or the whirr of his wings, flew back to urge Gisella and Nubia on. Even so, they couldn't keep up. They came to a small stream. They were thirsty, and Gisella put her muzzle into the water.

"Stop!" said a gurgling voice. "Don't drink me." It was the stream speaking. "I'm poisoned."

She looked into the stream and saw a horse's head staring up at her from the bottom. Looking upstream she saw its legs sticking stiffly into the air.

"Death and gasoline have poisoned me," said the stream. "If you drink me, you, too, will die." Gisella thanked the stream and, without drinking, they ran on.

They came to a road where they heard people, and they hid in the bushes. Along came a man and a woman nursing a baby, followed by three children and a bent, bearded man who looked older than Great-Aunt Tanteh. They were pulling a creaking cart full of things that could have belonged to Gisella's family except that the pictures in their battered frames had different faces. They spoke Crag with a Norland accent. From the opposite direction limped a young man on a crutch made from a forked tree limb. He had only one leg. He wore the ragged remains of a black Surland Army uniform. The family stopped and watched uneasily as he approached. He hopped up to them, and when he spoke Crag, they laughed with relief. He begged for food, and they gave him bread.

"You're going in the wrong direction," they said. "You must hide from our emperor's soldiers. They are killing our kind, old and young. The prison camps are full of Crags waiting to die."

"Well," said the young man, his mouth full of bread, "my own queen, Sydnia the Sweet, isn't too fond of us either. I joined her army to keep your emperor from taking my home-land. Before my first battle, our general called out all us Crag men. We were only about a dozen. He took away our guns.

"'Make the queen proud, boys!' he said. 'Show her you're not the mouse-hearted cowards everyone thinks you are. You go first! Sing one of your Craggy songs; we'll be right behind you!' My friend Tavido led the way. . . ."

Gisella almost leapt out to ask if it was her Tavido, her own dear brother. But she stopped herself, leaned forward, and pricked up her fox ears.

"At the first shot," the soldier continued, "my leg was gone and I fainted. When I opened my eyes, I found the rest of our group blown to bits. I couldn't tell one from the other."

Gisella stifled a scream. The family wept and shook their

heads. "The general and his army had run off like rats," the young man said. "They left me for dead, and if they find me now, they'll say, 'deserter!' and shoot me for sure. Both sides, while they fight each other, are using the war to get rid of the Crags."

"Why does everyone hate us?" one of the children asked.

"Who knows?" said the soldier. "Maybe it's because we cook our dumplings a little differently, or because we speak a different language, or because of the way we wear our hats . . . who knows?"

Everyone shrugged and shook their heads. The soldier and the family went off together.

Gisella heard Quick's hum and saw him flash across the road and into the woods. Had Tavido been blown to bits? She hadn't thought of him for days. Panic rattled her heart, but she leaped up and they all followed Quick.

On and on they went by day and by night, almost never stopping. Gisella didn't know how many days. They ate nothing, and they did not sleep. One early evening, they found themselves deep in a forest, in a small clearing under an old oak. They were exhausted, it was drizzling, and Quick had disappeared. April settled on a low branch to rest, and Nubia went off to hunt mice and squirrels. Gisella was worn out and heavy with worry. She lay down and wrapped her tail around her. Rain began to fall as if the woods were weeping.

Something woke her. It was barely dawn. Through the trees, the sky had cleared low in the East. Her nose twitched at something in the breeze: the scent of rain-soaked clover . . . a small meadow . . . a rabbit, male, fat . . . she could hear him chewing. She got to her feet.

10

Hunger took her over, and something wild that was more than hunger. She was a hungry fox and all the world was only hunger and the scent of the prey, and the need to make the distance between it and her jaws smaller and smaller, less and less, creeping like a shadow, becoming silence, hearing only the quickening beat of the prey's heart, until that perfect moment—the dash, the chase, the pounce, the scream, the crack of bone, and then . . . food. She made her first kill.

In her human form, Gisella had always loved small animals, and when she found one hurt or helpless, she cared for it. Now, as a fox, she found she loved them still, but in a different way. And she thanked the rabbit, limp in her jaws, for the great gift of its life. She dragged it back to the oak and found Nubia munching on a plump squirrel. April pecked for seeds and bugs. And so they dined together.

The breeze shifted and a fierce, rank odor filled the little clearing. Nubia caught it first and froze. Then he arched and hissed. April began to cluck and mutter, "Oh, my goodness! Oh, my goodness!"

Gisella turned and there, looking into the clearing, was a huge black bear.

"It's you again!" growled Nubia.

Gisella moved close to him and faced the bear, showed her teeth, and growled, too.

"I remember you, cat," said the bear. Gisella understood every word; a fox does know all languages, she thought. "I was at the trial," the bear continued. "I wouldn't want you for my lawyer! And, then again, that day I last spoke with Flame the fox—or the girl—or whatever she is now! I'll always remember that day. I ran from the monster in the sky, but it put something in my leg—thanks to her! It slows me, this thing; it pains me. I was a great forager and hunter. Now I'm always hungry. But I'm still strong—stronger than the both of you." And here he growled and looked at Gisella. "And you . . . what are you?" he snarled. "A girl that looks like a fox or a fox pretending to be a girl? I think I'll just take your head off and see what's really in there."

"What's he saying?" whispered Nubia. "I'm not good with bear talk."

Gisella spoke to the bear.

"I am not Flame. I am a girl named Gisella who's looking for her. She stole my body and I want it back. None of us needs

a fight, and there's food enough to share. Come, help yourself."
He looked at her doubtfully and sniffed the air.

"It's too strange," he said. "You look and smell like Flame,
but you talk like a girl speaking perfect bear . . . too strange."
He shuddered and limped his way to what was left of the
rabbit and squirrel and swallowed it. Gisella could see it was
less than a snack for him. She lifted her nose again and caught
a whiff of something. "Wait here," she said, and leapt into
the woods.

She went because she saw that he was starving and she
didn't want to be his dinner. But also, she had to admit to herself, for the pleasure of another hunt. She dragged back a fat
woodchuck and dropped it before the bear. It didn't last long.
The woods echoed with cracks and crunches as his jaws shattered the bones.

"Too many teeth!" worried April, staring down at him. She
had hopped from branch to branch high into the oak above
their heads. "I don't like things that are so big and have so
many teeth, the pointy kind. . . ."

"He's hurt, April," Gisella told her. "We must be kind. He
won't harm us." But, of course, she had no idea what he would
do. She wished Quick was with them. What if he disappeared
forever? What would they do then?

The bear licked his muzzle and his paws.

"Whatever you are," he said to her, "you've been kind and
I must repay you."

"No," she said. "It's all right."

"I must!" he growled. "It's the law."

"What law?" she asked him.

"The law that's written in my bones, of course. And in yours. . . ." He growled low. "But I have to keep reminding myself that you're not . . . that fox! How I hate her!"

"Because of the bullet in your leg?"

"Not only that. From before that."

"Why?"

"Why? I'll tell you why! We were born in the same woods, and ever since we were cubs . . . she teased me, taunted and tormented me! 'You're so slow!' she jeered. 'So stupid, so sloppy, so ugly . . .' She laughed at me! And I hate being laughed at. I chased her but could never catch her. And one day, chasing her, I fell into a trap and, oh, how she laughed then. And when men came and dragged me away, she laughed even harder! The men beat me and made me dance and put me in a circus where people came . . . and they laughed at me! Oh, how they laughed! Finally, I escaped back to the woods and there was Flame—'The clown is back!' she crowed. 'The stupid clown, the stinky clown!' I'd love to rip her guts out! I used to chase her all over the woods and make a fool of myself. Now I can hardly walk. I want her neck between my jaws!" He bared his teeth and snarled.

"You're scaring me," said Gisella.

"Sorry," he said.

"I hate her, too," she said, "and now she and my family are prisoners of the emperor. His flying machine put the bullet in you. We're going to find them and free them and I'll get my body back. Do you think I can make her give it back?"

"I will help you," said the bear. "Oh, if I get a hold of her, believe me, she'll give it back!"

If you get a hold of her, thought Gisella, what will be left of it! My poor body. This bear frightened her.

But she thought of being in her own body again, with her own family in their own house, and she began to cry. She imagined that somewhere, far out in the surrounding darkness—waiting for them—there was the warm glow of a happy ending. Somewhere. She had to reach it. And if it wasn't there, somehow, she had to make it be there.

Now the bear was snoring. She curled up with him and licked his wounded leg. After a minute, she snored, too.

11

Gisella was wakened by the whir of hummingbird wings. The morning was dark gray and wet. Quick hovered over a toadstool, took his true form, and shook the water from his hair.

"I've tried to go around the worst of the war, Gisella, but now we're close to Norland and the battle; today we'll be there. It's awful," he whispered, "and getting awfuller! This war is not like the last wars, the past wars where people simply chopped each other up. These things that explode like thunder . . . like lightning, and the roaring things full of gasoline— they're destroying my world! The invisible world is ripped full of enormous holes. You should see them! All the magic is bleeding away! My people are trying to save it—in boxes, bags, buckets, hats, pockets, baskets—but every day there's less and less . . . and without magic . . ." He shook his head. "We won't exist! My people and I will . . . will . . . vanish! You'll find us only in stories!" He shrugged hopelessly. "I'm not used to this kind of thing. To tell the truth . . . I'm frightened."

"Do we have a chance?" asked Gisella. "Will we make it?"

"Gisella," he said, "I was going to ask you the same question. . . ."

Gisella saw his eyes tremble. "Of course we'll make it," she said.

Quick sighed and looked away. "We'd better get started," he said, and he was a bird again.

"Please try to stay closer to us!" said Gisella, but he was already off into the wet gray woods and she didn't think he heard her.

"Nubia," called Gisella. "April, bear, come! We're off again!" A sleepy April fluttered down out of the tree, onto her back.

"Cock-a-doodle-do," she yawned. She had taken to crowing in the mornings. "Somebody has to do it," she said. When she saw the bear, she was very upset. "The mountain of fur with teeth! It's following us!"

"Stupid chicken!" he growled, and snapped at her as they started off. Gisella tried to reassure April that he was a friend, but she continued to glance nervously over her shoulder at him limping along behind them.

It began to rain. In the rattle and patter of water on leaves, Quick's small humming, how ever much Gisella strained to hear it, was soon lost.

"Quick!" she barked. "Why can't you stay close?"

It rained harder. Her fur became soaked. It was like being

wrapped in a cold, sopping-wet blanket. After what seemed hours, they emerged from the forest into open fields. Here, the rain beat down without mercy. A distance away, motionless in the downpour as if waiting for something, stood a small gray-hooded figure. They came up behind it and stopped.

The figure turned. It was the owl-faced person Gisella had met before. Flame's lawyer! Was it days ago, she wondered, or weeks or months? Behind the curtain of raindrops dripping from its hood, the owl-person blinked its huge yellow eyes.

"Aha!" it said. "A traveling circus! Bear and all!" There was a low growl, and April looked around and squawked. The bear sat right behind her, tongue hanging down, rain drumming his head.

"I hate circuses!" he growled. The owl-person seemed not to hear him.

"Won't the guards at the prison camp be pleased!" he said. "They love a circus. Even the emperor loves a circus. Takes his mind off the war. It's not going well, the war. Are you Norlanders or Surlanders?"

"We . . . we're . . . animals," Gisella stuttered.

"Of course, of course! You just don't want to be Crags, do you? No matter what kind of creatures you are. Not these days. Especially since they caught those spies, a whole family, can you imagine? Mother, grandfather, great-aunt, even the little girl—all spies!"

"A family?" cried Gisella "Have they been . . . are they safe?"

"They're in the prison camp. The old woman has something—something the emperor wants. . . . Don't you just love our emperor?" the owl-person rattled on. "In spite of his . . . odor? But we don't speak of that, do we? Of course, we don't! And so tell me about your circus—the bear dances, does he? And a dancing fox, oh, that's new! That's different! His Majesty will love that! Dare I ask . . . I mean, would you show me a bit of what you do? Just a few steps?"

Gisella began to wonder if this owl-person might be completely mad. Or was he trying to help them?

"Well, uh, s-sir . . . ," Gisella stammered, "unfortunately, we have no music, and really, we're a bit out of practice."

"That's right!" cried the owl-person. "Practice! Practice! Practice! Go ahead, just a few steps, a bit of a waltz. I'll keep time, you can sing along. Please! You can't refuse me! One two three, one two three . . . La laa la la laaah! La lah! Lalah!" There was a lightning flash. The thunder rumbled like a kind of music. The bear roared and rose up before Gisella—she jumped back, terrified. But then he did an awkward bow.

"Follow me," he said. "I know the waltz all too well, and I hate it and I hate the circus, but I will do it to help you." Gisella leaned into his fur, the smell of wet bear and the smell of wet fox mingled as he wrapped his forelegs around her. She was afraid he might crush her as they floundered and lurched in circles. But in a muddy field with the rain pouring down, Gisella learned to waltz. It wasn't easy, balancing on her hind legs in the mud. She teetered and stumbled in circles. She could hardly see for the rain. Nubia, caught up in the moment, leaped onto the bear's broad head and began to sing. April flapped up onto Nubia's back, turned circles, and crowed. Gisella could feel the bear's pain with each step they took, but he waltzed bravely. Nubia drowned out everything but the thunder with his yowling.

"Bravo!" cried the stranger, applauding enthusiastically. He stuck his little fingers in the corners of his mouth and emitted the most earsplitting whistles while he himself pranced in little circles in the mud. "Brilliant! Superb! The guards at the prison camp will adore you! The emperor, too! You may even 'knock them dead'! Do you know the expression? And . . . I have just what you need to absolutely ensure your success. . . ." From under his cloak he took a big leather suitcase.

From the suitcase he first pulled a long pole and stuck it in the mud. A large umbrella opened on top of it and he dragged Gisella beneath it.

"Here they are," he said. "Costumes!" With the rain drumming deafeningly down, he dressed her in clothes from the bag. Then he dressed the others in turn.

Nubia wore a broad-brimmed black felt hat with a peacock feather, a green jacket with tails, and big yellow leather boots.

April wore a little straw hat and a gingham apron. The owl somehow stuffed the poor bear into a pink satin tutu and put huge ballet slippers of the same material on his hind paws. Gisella was in a scarlet hunter's jacket and top hat. How awful it felt to be in clothes! Especially wet. How did she stand it when she was human? she wondered. The whole thing had a feel of unreality, but they looked like a circus.

"Don't worry about paying for these," said the stranger. "I'll wait till you make your fortunes! It was an honor to have met you! A privilege!" He shook paws and claws all around. "Good luck!" he said, and splashed off into the rain.

"Bless you, sir!" Gisella called after him. "Thank you! For everything!" She laughed and shook the rain and mud from her coat. "What luck!" she cried to the others. "Whoever that was, he told and gave us all we need. My family is still alive! We know where they are. We can save them! We are now a circus!"

"With my singing," said Nubia, "we might even become an opera."

"And I," crowed April, "might become a rooster!"

"I hate circuses," growled the bear, and then limped silently along behind as they plunged on into the storm and across the fields.

12

They saw people moving toward them through the rain. Families, some with wheelbarrows, some pulling carts. Many women with children. The sound of wailing babies threaded through the downpour. Soon the fields were streaming with people by the hundreds. All Crags. Tablecloths and blankets held over their heads. Most passed them with hardly a glance except for the children. They called out and laughed and waved. Some pointed and said, "Look, Mommy, a bear! A fox!"

Gisella heard a young man singing. His voice was beautiful, loud and clear. It reminded her of Tavido. It was an old Crag song:

> *I sing the far mountains*
> *Where bold eagles fly.*
> *Reach out your fingers*
> *And tickle the sky. . . .*

"Shhhh!" people around him hissed. "You're crazy!" The boy kept singing. Other young men joined in:

The air tastes of freedom
The wind sings of love,
All the world lies below . . .
Only heaven above
I'll meet you there!
I'll take you there!

"They are killing people for singing such songs!" a man shouted.

"And not just the soldiers," added a woman. "Our neighbors are killing us! Our grocers are killing us!"

"They say we are all spies, like the family they caught—the old lady with the chickens."

"It's time to defend ourselves!" cried the singer. "It's time to fight back! Join us!"

"You're right," called someone else. "What have we got to lose?"

"I'm with you!" shouted another. "We should have our own country!"

"Yes! A Crag country!" shouted someone else.

"Join us!" shouted others. "All of you!" More singers joined the chorus:

I sing of the mountains,
Where we tickle the sky,
We dream of the mountains,
And the times long gone by. . . .

Many people moved away from the singers. But a growing group—men and women, young and old—sang and raised their fists and cried, "We must fight for ourselves! We must make our own country! Join us!" A loud, nasty buzzing interrupted.

A huge screaming black thing flew low out of the clouds. It was Gisella's first sight of an aeroplane. People looked up and began to run. An explosion nearby threw up a geyser of mud, and there were screams. Here and there, along with the rain, bombs fell. The singers sang louder and marched on through them. Between bomb blasts Gisella heard the *thump* and *boom* of artillery. She and her friends couldn't move because of all the people, and just stood still as the refugees ran frantically around them. After a while, the crowds thinned, and the bombing stopped. In the distance behind her, Gisella heard the singing fade. A bent old woman with a bundle on her back was the last to pass. Then Gisella and her circus marched on to Norland alone.

13

The thud of cannons and the rattle of gunfire encircled them. The rain had stopped, but the clouds hung low and looked dirty, like old quilts losing their stuffing. A wind full of evil smells blew hard in their faces, and all along the horizon ran a jagged scribble of barbed wire on wooden posts—the Norland border.

Directly ahead was a little guardhouse, like a privy with red and white barber stripes. Standing next to it, watching the circus approach, were two Norland soldiers with rifles. Even at a distance they looked scared.

"Halt!" one of them shouted. Both aimed their rifles at Gisella and the others.

"Cock-a-doodle-do," said April, not knowing what else to say. The soldiers lowered their rifles. The bear stood on his hind legs, and the rifles sprang up again.

"Approach slowly!" warned the soldiers. And so Gisella did. The soldiers whistled and cursed in amazement when they got close. One of them, not much older than Gisella, puffed a cigar. They were only boys with helmets and dirty uniforms that were too big. They circled the bedraggled circus suspiciously and scanned the distance in all directions.

"Just animals," said the cigar smoker, "dressed better than we are. . . . Where's the people?"

The other one shrugged. "Maybe it's some dirty enemy trick."

Gisella stood up and bowed to the bear. He managed a curtsy, and they went into their waltz, with Nubia and April doing their parts. Without the rain and on firmer ground, they did much better than the first time.

"Look at that!" cheered the boys, laughing and jumping up and down. "They're great! Again! Come on! Do it again!" The performers did an encore and added little touches as they gained confidence. The cheering was even wilder.

"This is a circus!" yelled the young soldiers. "We got a whole circus here!" They hugged each other and did their own little dance.

"We could make some money with this! We could make a lot!"

"A whole lot! Bring 'em to the prison camp! Put on a show for the guards!"

"They won't believe it!"

"They'll fall over! I heard even the emperor likes a circus!"

"I'll take 'em to the camp; you guard the border."

"Oh, no! I'll take 'em!" said the one with the cigar.

"It'll be me!" warned the other, raising his rifle.

"Okay, okay! We both take 'em! Hell with the border!"

"Hell with the border!" said the other. "The war's lost anyway! Everybody says so. . . ."

They raised the wooden barrier, opened the big barbed-
wire gate, and herded the circus through into Norland. With
one boy leading and the other following, they crossed a stone
bridge over a river and into the outskirts of the capital city.

Shutters were closed. Shops boarded up. The streets were
empty.

Just as they turned onto the road to the prison camp, the
sun slid from behind a cloud and lit up the hill above the town.
Nothing in Gisella's life had prepared her for what she saw.
There, reflecting rainbows in every direction, stood a palace
made all of crystal. She stopped and stared.

"Keep going!" cried one of the boys. "First the camp, then
the palace!"

"Yes! With these animals, we'll actually get inside the
Crystal Palace!"

"When the emperor sees our circus, he'll make us rich!"
said the other. "Filthy rich!"

They continued on while the young soldiers talked excitedly of all they'd do with their money. From the top of a small

hill, Gisella looked down at a vast puddled wasteland of mud surrounded by a very high fence of barbed wire.

It was the prison camp. Hundreds of people stood inside, not moving, not talking, faces gray, silent. A dreadful stink of filth, sickness, hunger, fatigue, terror, and hopelessness hung over them. It frightened Gisella and made her want to weep. Above the big double gates was a sign: "All Crags Welcome!" Guards came out of the little houses on either side. Some pointed their guns at the strange parade; some just stared.

"Halt!" shouted a bald sergeant, brown as leather. "What's your business here?"

"Sir!" cried the boys. "The circus is in town!" The sergeant stared at them and then at Gisella and her friends.

"Who's guarding the border?" he demanded. The boys turned pale, looked at each other and then at the ground.

"No one, sir, but . . ."

"No one? *No one*, you say? You left your country—your beloved Norland—unguarded to bring us a circus? *Deserters!*"

He snatched the boys up by their collars, knocked their heads together several times, and with kicks and curses, threw them to guards who dragged them away. So much for their riches and dreams, thought Gisella. Then, with fists on his hips, the sergeant turned his attention to the animals. The rest of the guards moved closer.

"Well," he said, "I wonder what it is they do, exactly."

Gisella and the bear began their routine again. Each time they performed, Gisella hated it more: the binding costumes, the eyes staring at her. But now she was a professional, danc-ing for her family's life. The sergeant's eyes opened wide. The soldiers oohed and aahed, laughed and applauded.

"Someone play some music!" ordered the grinning sergeant as he clapped in time. "Where's Eric with his accordion?"

"Dead," someone answered.

"How 'bout Georgy and his flute?"

"Hands blown off yesterday," someone else said.

"Dammit! There should be music with this! This is amaz-ing! Can't somebody play something?" bellowed the sergeant.

And then, like a miracle, the clear, sweet sound of a violin floated out over the camp. It was an old Crag waltz. The sounds of war disappeared. At first, Gisella couldn't believe it. Then her heart filled with joy. There was only one fiddle that sounded like that. Her father's. And only one person in the whole world who could play it like that. Tavido!

The soldiers cheered, sang, and hummed along, and as Gisella stepped and turned, she saw, just behind the barbed wire, her brother, playing the violin, a bloody bandage over his eyes. Her mother stood on one side of him, her grandfather on the other, and next to him stood Flame. The fox in Gisella's body stared at her.

Now Gisella danced with all her heart. There was hope!

Here was her family; here was her true body. Even the crowds behind the barbed wire brightened. She heard children laugh. The smell of despair began to fade. The sky had cleared, and a sweet golden light came from the lowering sun. They danced and capered on and on till everyone was singing and cheering and the last light turned to night. A lieutenant on horseback had joined the audience, and when darkness ended the performance and the last applause had died away, he shouted, "Sergeant!"

"Sir!" said the sergeant with a salute and a click of his heels.

"Bring these"—he pointed to Gisella and her circus—"animals to the palace in the morning! The musician, too. Ten o'clock sharp! For the emperor!"

"Sir!" cried the sergeant as the officer galloped off. The little circus was locked in a yard with the horses and given food and water. The bear, Nubia, and April all slept. But Gisella couldn't sleep. The yard was next to the camp fence. She paced along it back and forth for hours, till, glancing up, she saw Flame behind the fence looking back at her.

14

"I want my body!" hissed Gisella. "Now!"

Flame looked between the strands of barbed wire, into Gisella's eyes, and smiled. The night was dark, but to a fox, darkness is another kind of light. Gisella returned her look.

"Are you sure?" Flame asked coolly. Is that my voice, wondered Gisella? Is that my face? Or are they becoming Flame's?

"Are you sure you want to be in here?" said Flame. "Starving? Waiting to die? How would that help your family?" Gisella quickly looked away, and Flame laughed. Maybe Flame is right, thought Gisella, but she so longed to be with her loved ones; isn't that where she was supposed to be? Yes, and when they were together, everything would be all right! She looked back into Flame's eyes.

"Are you really sure?" Flame asked again. Gisella hesitated. Again she looked away. Flame was right. It was Gisella who had to save her family. Should they all die because she couldn't wait to be with them? Wouldn't even try to help them?

"And why," Flame continued slyly, "why I would trade places with you now? I may look human but I'm not completely stupid! A circus clown? Wearing those ridiculous clothes? Locked up with that fat-headed bear—I could never resist teasing him, poor thing; he's so funny when he's angry. Oh, no! Tomorrow when they take you to perform for the emperor, you must find a way to get us out of here! Then we'll think about changing bodies. This place is horrible! Now I know why humans have such poor noses—the stinks they have to live with! Are war and prison camps someone's idea of fun? Being human could be fun all the time—you have fingers and chickens and music and families. I like your family; Great-Aunt Tanteh knows so much. . . ."

"Where is she?" Gisella cried. She had almost forgotten about her great-aunt.

"She's in the palace. The emperor is doing awful things to her; no other creature would do such things to its own kind— or any other kind. He wants her to tell him how to make December lay golden eggs. There are two things I will never understand: Why people hate Crags—I know why they hated me as a fox . . . but as a Crag? And why do they love gold? Can you explain it to me? They can't eat it and yet they kill for it; it's nice to look at, but so are flowers. So is the moon. If anything human is precious, it's music! That's the secret I want!"

"All right!" said Gisella. "I will find a way to free all of us. Then we must change back. You must promise!"

"Free us," said Flame as she turned and strolled into the darkness. "Then we'll see."

Gisella's head was whirling with awful thoughts: What were they doing to Great-Aunt Tanteh? How would she free everyone? What could a bunch of poor animals really do? Where was their plan? She'd never felt so helpless.

Then she thought of Tavido and Grandpa and her mother. Even though they were separated, she felt they were still connected somehow, they were close to her—how could that be? Of course! Love connected them. It would always connect them. She would find a way.

She slept briefly and dreamed of birds flying. Thousands of them. Birds of every kind and size and color. Each singing a different song. All flying home.

They were wakened at dawn by guards with more food and water, and Tavido was led into their pen. Gisella was overwhelmed by a mix of pain and joy. He was blind. He had the fiddle and bow in one hand and a long stick in the other to feel his way. She ran to him, licked his hand, leapt up to his chest, and ran circles around him.

"Tavido! Dear Tavido!" she cried, but he heard only yelps and barks. He was startled at first, but then he laughed and rubbed her head and knelt so she could kiss and lick his dear face.

"Is this a fox or a dog?" he laughed. "She's so tame! I think she likes me. Good fox! Sweet fox. . . ."

"Be careful," said a girl's voice. "You can never really trust a fox." Flame stepped out from behind him. She looked even less familiar in the morning light. I have to get my body back, thought Gisella, before it becomes completely hers! Around Flame's neck hung a small drum. Tavido had convinced the sergeant that, to perform for the emperor, they would need a drummer, and that Flame was a good one. Of course, she'd never seen a drum before. She winked at Gisella, and then stuck out her tongue and crossed her eyes at the bear. He roared, reared up, and took a swipe at her. One of the startled guards fell backward, while another aimed his rifle at the bear.

"Please!" Gisella barked to the bear. "That's my body she's wearing!"

The bear backed off. "The last laugh," he said to Flame, "will be mine!" She just snickered and took Tavido's hand.

When Nubia came to rub against his legs, Tavido recognized his voice, and with his hands, knew him for sure. And April also. He was overjoyed and amazed to find them there.

"But where did they get clothes?" he wondered. "And how did they join up with a fox and a bear to become a circus?"

How can I tell him? thought Gisella. How can I let him know who I really am?

"My dear son, my dearest daughter," came a tearful voice. "May you be safe!" Gisella's mother stood behind the barbed wire next to Gisella's grandfather. Gisella ran up to her, yelping and barking, throwing herself against the wire. She longed to be in her mother's arms. How could she not be in her arms? How could her own mother not know her? But her mother's eyes were startled and full of fear. The guards knocked Gisella away. She tried to bite them, but one stunned her with his rifle butt and they got a rope around her neck.

The sergeant gave orders. They lined the circus up and surrounded them with guards.

Mother and Grandpa waved from behind the barbed wire.

"Don't worry," Tavido called to them in Crag. "I think, with these animals, we'll find a way out of here!"

"Good luck!" they yelled back, and off the circus went.

It was only then that Gisella noticed how quiet it was. The guns had stopped. Was the war over?

As they went through the capital, they passed more and more soldiers and cannons behind bags of sand piled into high walls that lined the streets leading up the hill. Sharpshooters looked down at them from the rooftops.

The closer they got to the Crystal Palace, which was flashing and sparkling, the more it seemed to be made of light. The air around it was rainbow colored, and there was a tinkling like thousands of wind chimes. At the palace gates, which were also crystal and decorated with glass vines and fruit, stood tall, fierce-looking guards all in purple. Just as the circus came up to the gates, they swung open. Out rode a general with red mustachios on a white horse.

At the sight of the circus, the horse, eyes rolling, neighed wildly and rose on its hind legs. The general yelped, fell backward, and landed with a splash in a puddle of muddy water. The guards covered their mouths, turned crimson, and shook, while the general's aides rushed to help him up and brush him off.

"Who is responsible"—he demanded through clenched teeth—"for this . . . zoo?"

"Sir!" cried the sergeant saluting and clicking his heels. "The circus is here to entertain the emperor!"

One of the general's aides gave him a little lens, which he put in his eye.

"A circus!" he said, looking them over. "Well . . . what a good idea. The emperor needs some entertainment. Yes! During the cease-fire. For the meeting with the queen. A little entertainment will keep them . . . occupied. Take them to the emperor!"

He stepped aside and they were marched through the gates. They crossed a crystal bridge over a moat. Gisella was startled to see that it was full of snakes, crocodiles, and vile scurrying things she had never seen before or since. She shuddered. They went up crystal stairs and into the Crystal Palace.

15

They were marched through vast mirrored corridors—walls, ceilings, and floors all mirrors. They (except for poor Tavido) saw themselves reflected above and below and on both sides into infinity. Tinkling sounds came from countless complicated crystal chandeliers. Gisella almost didn't hear the tiny voice that whispered, "Gisehh-laaaa. . . ."

"Quick!" she whispered back. "Where are you? I thought we'd lost you forever!"

From the top of her head, no bigger than a gnat, Quick scurried down to the tip of her nose.

"Gisella," he said, "I've got to get away from here! This palace is not safe for me! Humans can see me in mirrors—especially mirrors reflected in mirrors! And the invisible world is gone! It's been blown to bits and the bits blown to nothing, and where it was . . . there's just a hole in the world! It was so beautiful and we'll never see it again! And all my people are gone—I'm the only one left. They've taken the last of the magic and flown off somewhere so distant, so hidden, and so unknown, I don't think I'll be able to find it! I have just a little magic left, Gisella. . . . I want to help you—I have to help you—but I am alone and lost and scared!"

Looking cross-eyed at him on the tip of her nose, she saw two of him, weeping and wringing his tiny hands. She forgot her own fear.

"Dear Quick, everything will come out right," she whispered. What else could she say? "We are a circus now, and everyone says circuses always have happy endings. Now, hide in my ear and please tell me . . . did you find Great-Aunt Tanteh? Is she all right?"

He crawled into her ear.

"It's cozy in here," he sobbed. "I could live here happily and never come out. I have heard weeping and screaming. I've heard clucking and muttering. But I haven't found which dungeon she is in. Under the palace it's all a mirrored maze with mirrored chambers where the tortured must watch themselves suffer. . . ."

"Halt!" said one of the guards. "The emperor's office!" They were in front of a great mirrored door. Their guard whispered something to the guard at the door, who knocked and whispered something to a guard inside, who opened the door, whispered something back, and closed it again. But before it closed, Gisella caught a whiff of something very odd and unpleasant—and she heard a chicken clucking.

"We're in luck!" said April brightly. "The emperor is a chicken!"

"That's December in there," whispered Nubia. "I'd know her cluck anywhere."

"You're right!" said April. "How did December get to be the emperor?"

Their guard turned to them. "The emperor is in confer-ence," he said. "I must take you to the waiting room." He marched them down another corridor.

"Maybe Great-Aunt Tanteh is in there, too!" Gisella whispered. "We have to find out. Quick, are you still in my ear?"

"I'm not sure," said a tiny voice. "What do you want?"

"Just creep under the emperor's door," she said. "See what's going on. It'll be easy."

"Easy to be squashed!" he squeaked. "Smashed! Squished!"

"You must," she said.

"I know," he sighed. "I must."

He became a moth, fluttered out of her ear, and was gone.

The waiting room had big windows that gave a view of the city and its walls. Beyond them, they could see the muddy fields they had crossed that morning. But now the fields were covered with hundreds of the monstrous armored wagons with their guns all pointed at the palace, and behind them, a glitter-ing restless dark mass—the queen's army, all in black, had sur-rounded the city. While they waited, Tavido tried to teach

Flame to play her drum, but it was difficult for her. She got too excited; she would begin, listen to her own beating, and forget to play. Tavido was patient, but she became angry and threw her drumsticks on the floor.

"Gisehh-laaaa!" Quick's voice was again in her ear. She hadn't noticed his return.

"Listen!" he said. "I crawled under a door into a room mirrored like the rest of the palace except that these mirrors magnify everything so that everyone looks even more enormous and hideous than they really are—and tiny as I make myself, there's more chance of my being seen! There, I found the emperor. He smells like onions and coffee and skunk and lily of the valley and dead fish and many other things that I couldn't identify. He looks like a purple barrel decorated with medals; his little head sticks up on top like a spigot. He and a smaller man, the assistant emperor I think, sat on the floor and tickled a chicken who didn't want to be tickled. She escaped their grasp and fluttered around the room, leaving droppings everywhere she could, especially on the two men. On the table, there was a golden egg.

"'It's been weeks and she's laid only one egg,' said the emperor sulkily, 'and that one only for the old Crag hag who won't tell us the secret no matter what we do to her.' He picked up a sword, slipped it from its scabbard, and looked at the chicken. 'I am itching to slit this bird open and see exactly where those eggs come from.'

"'A daring thought, your majesty!' said the assistant. 'Very tempting.'

"'Yes,' said the emperor, and sighed. 'But what I've learned is that things rarely work as well when you try to put them back together again.' He put away the sword and sat slumped on the floor. He began to chew his thumbnail.

"'What shall we do? Here we are, out of bullets, out of soldiers, and out of money, surrounded by that loathsome queen's incompetent army, and just because she has hundreds of motorized tanks, she has the nerve to demand my absolute surrender or, she says, she'll blow my palace to bits! My Crystal Palace! One of the wonders of the world—took twenty years to build, millions in gold, and thousands of glass blowers—and that ninny wants to blow it to bits! Now . . . if I had a perpetual supply of golden eggs, I could buy new armies, bigger guns, aeroplanes, battleships, submarines, gasoline! I could rule the world!'

"'You could, Your Majesty!' said his assistant. 'You would. What's your plan?'

"'My plan? Do you think I don't have one?'

"'Oh, no, Your Majesty, I know you have an excellent plan, an infallible plan, one that's way beyond my poor muddled mind. . . .'

"'Of course I do! Guess! Guess what it is!'

"'Well,' said the assistant, 'hmm . . . the old hag . . . are you going to promise to let her and her wretched Crag family go if she tells the secret, and then, when she tells, have them all . . . eradicated?'

"'Good guess!' cried the emperor. 'Exactly! Have the hag brought up immediately!'

Orders were given, and in came a tall guard carrying a large wicker basket by its handle. He put it on the floor and left.

"In the basket sat an old, old woman all curled up small, very pale, her flickering eyes deep and dark as night. The black hen ran to her and hopped into her lap.

"'We have decided,' said the emperor, 'in our infinite good-ness, and against our better judgment, even though you are a spy and a filthy Crag enemy of my empire, to let you and your family go free and live wherever you like . . . if you tell us the secret of the golden eggs.'

"The old woman clucked softly. Or it might have been the hen. 'Do you promise?' She barely breathed the words.

"'Cross my heart,' said the emperor, but behind his back his fingers were crossed also. The hen and the old woman seemed to chuckle, and I was startled when she looked up—I'm sure she looked right at me, a speck on the chandelier—and winked! I nearly lost my grip.

"'Very well.' The old woman nodded and chuckled again. She spoke so very softly, the two men, to catch every word, moved closer and knelt before her basket.

"'It's simple . . . you just say,

Little black hen,
of thee I beg,
pray thee,
lay me
a golden egg.'

" 'That's all?' said the emperor and his assistant.

" 'Yes, but . . . you must say it in the secret language of the birds. Like this . . .' And she cackled and muttered, wheezed and whistled, and the hen cackled and ruffled her feathers, and the old woman reached under her and brought out a golden egg. The emperor snatched it. 'How can I learn the secret language of the birds?' he cried impatiently.

" 'Simple,' muttered the old woman. 'Find a crow's nest full of eggs. Take the eggs, and boil them till they are hard. Replace them in the nest. When the mother crow returns and finds the hard-boiled eggs, she will fly off to the Red Sea. On its shore, she will pick up a stone with her beak. She will fly back and touch her eggs with the stone and they will become fresh again. Take that stone, touch it to your tongue, and you will speak the secret language of the birds.'

"The emperor and his assistant stared at the old woman for a moment; then they looked at each other.

" 'And then the hen will lay golden eggs?' asked the emperor.

" 'All you want,' whispered the old woman, and she closed her eyes.

"There was a pounding at the door.

" 'What is it? I'm busy!' shouted the emperor.

" 'The queen, Your Majesty,' said the guard. 'She's on her way!'

" 'Stall her!' the emperor told his assistant. 'I'll join you in the Great Conference and Circus Room!' The assistant hurried out and the emperor turned back to the old woman. He shook her basket roughly.

" 'Where do I find a crow's nest?' he demanded. The woman and the hen both chuckled.

" 'Far, far away,' said the woman, without opening her eyes. 'The birds are all flown from the war. End the war. I'll call them back. You'll have your golden eggs.'

" 'The war?' said the emperor. 'The war is over! I'm sick and tired of it. Bored to death! I'm going now to talk peace with Queen Sydnia the Sweet of Surland. Call the birds! The sooner the better!'

" 'Bring me,' said the old woman, 'my rooster, Gabriel. He shall call the birds.'

"The emperor opened the door and ordered the guard to bring the rooster, and that's when I flew out. Just past his nose, he grabbed me out of the air. He had me! Somehow—I don't know how—I slipped out of that loathsome fist . . . and here I am." Quick shuddered; Gisella felt it deep in her ear.

"Thank you, Quick," she whispered. "You are very brave."

The door flew open, and there stood their guards.

"*Show time!*" they shouted, and Gisella and the others were marched down the hall to the Great Conference and Circus Room.

16

The Great Conference and Circus Room was huge and circular, with open arched windows all around it. It was not mirrored, but of clear crystal, the ceiling a dome of crystal, so the blue sky spread above the little circus and they could see the countryside all around and, of course, the black swarm of the queen's army. Before them sat the emperor on a crystal throne, and next to him on the floor, a big wicker basket. In the basket, looking smaller and paler, her eyes deeper and darker than Gisella remembered, sat Great-Aunt Tanteh, and in her lap sat December and Gabriel, side by side.

"Kneel," intoned the guard, "before your emperor, Ignatz the XI, known for good reason as 'The Powerful,' ruler of Norland, Weyland, Eyeland, and Inner Myopia." They all did as he said. The emperor's odor was the smell of good things gone bad: peaches, bananas, eggs, roses, cheese. It was vile.

"Oh, excellent!" cried the emperor. "A circus! The queen is about to arrive, and we can all use a bit of fun!"

And sure enough, the doors were thrown open, the circus was pushed to the side, and the guard chanted, "All welcome Her Majesty, Queen Sydnia, known as 'The Sweet,' ruler of Surland, Yurland, Mieland, and Outer Myopia." Four armed bearers in black entered carrying a black platform and, standing on it, a short, stocky woman in black with a pasty white face. On her head was an evil-looking crown sprouting long, sharp bronze spikes. She pointed a long black sword straight at the emperor with one hand and held her nose with the other.

"Surrender, you stinking dog!" she bellowed. "Or I'll chop you to bits and blast your silly palace into ground glass!"

"Sydnia, Sydnia!" said the emperor, smiling and rising, his arms outstretched. "My dear! I'd forgotten how lovely—truly ravishing—you really are! Oh, I'm so bored with this stupid war—it was the Crags who made me do it! I never wanted to conquer your queendoms, only your heart! Come, my dear, and join our realms together. Marry me!"

The queen almost fell off her platform.

"I thought you were simply stupid," she said incredulously, "not completely insane! I could marry a goat or a pig . . . or a skunk! Why would I want to marry you?"

"Because, my dear, I adore you and all your queendoms, which, when combined with my empire, would constitute almost all of the entire Old Country; we could then exterminate all the Crags, blame them for everything, and live happily ever after on my endless supply of . . . golden eggs."

The queen lowered her sword, looked down at him, and said, "What golden eggs?"

"These golden eggs." He held up one in each hand. She let go of her nose and snatched an egg. She examined it closely and then cracked it on one of her bearers' helmets. The mercury ran down and the golden yolk rested on top.

"Keep it my love," crooned the emperor. "Only I—and this filthy old Crag hag—know the secret of obtaining them. End the war, marry me, and share the world and the riches! Fifty-fifty."

The queen looked down at him, sniffed the air.

"Eighty-twenty!" she said, nose again pinched firmly between her fingers.

"Sixty-forty!" cried the emperor.

"Seventy-thirty!"

The emperor turned a purple that matched his uniform. He wheedled and blustered, he flattered and spluttered, but finally, he agreed. The scribe was called. The treaty and all its terms and conditions were written on a long parchment curled up at the ends, and both sovereigns signed it.

"The war is over!" cried a bugle-like voice that startled everyone. It was Gabriel, the rooster. He was perched on the handle of Great-Aunt's basket. He flapped to a window and called again and again, "The war is over! The war is over! Come home! Come home!"

In her basket, Great-Aunt Tanteh, her eyes closed, grinned a wide, toothless grin.

"Most amazing!" said the queen. "A talking rooster!" Gisella wondered how it was the queen could understand him.

"I understood him also!" said the surprised emperor. "He's calling all the birds back." He turned to Great-Aunt Tanteh. "How does this bird speak? More of your Crag witchcraft?"

"This room," she answered, "is built over an ancient cross-roads between the worlds. It's a bubble of magic, the last one not destroyed by the war. Animal and human, visible and invisible—here, everyone can understand and see everyone else."

"I had no idea!" chortled the emperor. "Right in my own palace. And will the birds be here soon?"

"Very soon."

"And will there be crows among them?"

"There will"

"Excellent! Guards! Throw the hag out the window! I don't need her anymore!"

But there was no Great-Aunt for the guards to throw. Now, in the basket, there were two identical coal black hens.

"She's turned herself into a chicken!" cried the emperor. "You see? You can't trust a Crag! Which of you," he demanded of the hens, "is the real one?"

"I think it is I," said one of them. "Or should I say 'me'?"

"It's actually me!" said the other. "Or should I say 'I'?"

"It is either I or me or you," said the first.

"Or you or me or I," said the second.

"Unless it's someone else," said the first.

"This is utter nonsense!" the queen boomed at the emperor. "More of your treacherous tricks!"

"Listen!" It was Tavido, his face turned upward. "Listen. . . ."

There was a distant sound like a rising wind, like fluttering leaves, like an ocean coming closer. All around the horizon a cloud was rising. Gray at first, it was growing blacker.

"They're coming!" said Gabriel.

"The birds?" asked the emperor and queen together.

"The jury!" Gabriel crowed.

17

"The jury?" said the emperor. "This is a circus! What do we want a jury for?"

"For your trial," said the rooster. "Yours and the queen's."

"Trial?" said the queen. "Where is the court? Where is the judge who can try us? We are the law!"

"It's just a circus, my dear," laughed the emperor. "A mock trial to amuse us! On with the show!"

It was becoming dark and getting darker. Clouds made of birds were filling the sky overhead. The sound of millions of flapping wings grew louder and louder till it became a tremendous shuddering roar. A crow landed on the glass dome of the ceiling and looked down at everyone, and then another and another. And then starlings and sparrows and robins and others—more than could be identified or counted—all landed and the sky was clear, but they were under a dome of living birds that plunged the room into a kind of twilight. Then it was very still.

"Order in the court," said a small voice. It was like a whisper of wind, but each word rang in that vast domed space. Gisella saw a dot of light descending from the middle of the ceiling. It was the pure white spider lowering on its thread. It stopped high above the two rulers and seemed to float in the air. They stared at it, openmouthed, speechless, like two fishes.

Around the room, as they had at Flame's trial, animals appeared: snakes, deer, raccoons, toads, and others too numerous to mention; moths, butterflies, beetles, and bugs of every color and design watched from the walls.

Seated on the floor, perched on the chandeliers, and hovering in the air were sprites—large and small, old and young—and elves, fairies, nymphs, pixies, wraiths, and other kinds of invisible beings Gisella had never seen before.

"My people!" said Quick's voice in her ear. "They've come for the trial!"

The emperor looked annoyed and a little unsure. "This is not amusing me!" he croaked. "Guards! Throw these creatures out! Guards?"

"Where are the guards?" demanded the queen. She glared wildly about till she saw them cowering, eyes wide with terror, under the chairs. "Come out!" she raged. "Come out and do something!" But they only shrank farther back under their chairs.

"Is the jury assembled?" asked the spider.

"*We are!*" thundered all the birds that had landed on the dome and roofs and grounds of the palace.

"They are, Your Honor," croaked the crow.

"Lawyer for the prosecution come forward!" In through a window hopped the owl-person in his gray cloak. He waddled to the center and bowed.

"Your Honor," he said, "birds of the jury, we will prove beyond a feather of a doubt that this queen and this emperor have committed countless crimes, including inflicting tremendous damage on the visible world and the total destruction of the invisible world—a major source of magic—and they have purposely caused terrible pain and suffering to the creatures of both these worlds. Their behavior was wasteful, cruel, vicious, nasty, evil, and just plain mean!"

"How do you plead?" the spider asked the emperor and queen.

"We don't!" cried the emperor, standing up straight and stiff. "This court has no power! You're just a bunch of animals and bugs . . . and the rest of you are imaginary!"

"We are sovereign rulers!" said the queen, waving her sword. "What you don't seem to understand is that what we do is neither right nor wrong; it's history! And it will be written in books and studied long after all of you are gone and forgotten!"

"Prosecution," said the spider, "call your witnesses."

"First witness," said the owl. "State your name and what you saw."

After a moment's pause, Quick fluttered out of Gisella's ear and took his own shape in the middle of the room. He was no bigger than a grain of rice. He spoke, but was so tiny he couldn't be heard.

"Would the witness please enlarge himself?" asked the spider. Quick began to inflate like a balloon. In seconds he was twenty feet tall and getting taller.

"Say when, Your Honor."

"When!" said the judge. Quick, like a giant carved of living jade, now towered over the two rulers, who seemed to shrink and turn paler.

His voice rang in the crystal of all the chandeliers as he sang of the destruction of the invisible world and the bleeding away of the magic.

"Your Honor, I used to live in a perfect but fragile world just inside of this one, like the silk lining of an eggshell. The cities were made of sunbeams and moonbeams welded into towers of light connected by rainbow bridges, and all the curtains and hangings were woven from the shadows of twilight and dawn. We breathed an atmosphere of magic that radiated from spring meadows and deep woods, the songs of birds, the buzz of bees, the fall of rain and snow, and the happy dreams of infants.

"Then the armies, without even meaning to, without caring what was destroyed as they went about destroying each other, blasted, smashed, and completely obliterated our world—its atmosphere has bled away and we, the sprites, elves, fairies, pixies, and nymphs who lived there, are forced to breathe your air full of poison and pain, fear and grief, without a trace of magic, and we are dying, vanishing, lost—we are refugees without a refuge, wanderers wandering the farthest, emptiest spaces, looking for a hint of magic to keep us alive and from which to make a new world before we fade away . . . completely. I have seen things that I wish I hadn't and that I can never forget nor ever forgive and—please excuse me . . . I'm fading . . . fading . . ." And he was fading, becoming transparent and wavering. "I'm going to hide some more . . . maybe forever. . . ." In an eye-blink, he shrank, and flew back into Gisella's ear.

"Dear Quick," she said to him. Deep in her ear she felt his sobs.

The next witness was Tavido.

"I am a proud Surland Crag," he said, "who was willing to give my life for my country and queen. But she sent me and all my Crag comrades into battle armed only with our songs. Fortunately, I'm still alive; unfortunately, I'll never see my country or my family or anything again."

A sparrow told of how, when the war smashed their eggs, she and all the other birds were forced to fly far, far away.

Great-Aunt Tanteh resumed her original form and told what

had been done to her to get her secret. Gisella covered her ears with her paws.

A brook told of how it was poisoned by death and gasoline.

An oak tree told of how its forest was blasted into splinters.

Then everyone listened to several hours of empty silence, which was the testimony of a few of the thousands of dead. That was the worst.

"I rest my case," said the owl-person, bowing again to the court.

"Lawyer for the defense come forward," said the judge. No one moved. No one spoke. Everyone looked around.

"Is there no one who will defend the accused?" asked the judge. "Are there no lawyers here?"

"Your Honor," said Nubia, leaping into the center, "I am a lawyer, and in spite of this short notice, and the fact that I find the accused loathsome and their deeds despicable, I will take the case!"

"Thank you. Call your first witness."

"I call Gisella, the girl in the body of a fox because her own body was stolen by the same fox, Flame, whom we accuse of theft and trickery!"

"I only borrowed her body!" shouted Flame, who was standing next to Tavido. "Just to see what it was like!"

"I thought so!" cried Tavido. "Dear Gisella! Even as a fox, somehow, I knew it was you!"

"Order in the court!" said the spider. "That is another case for another trial. Let us finish the matter at hand. Witness for the defense, please take the stand." Hesitantly, Gisella trotted to the center.

"What can you tell us," Nubia asked her, pacing back and forth, "about the emperor and queen?"

"I've never met them," she answered. "I have nothing to say."

"Have you ever heard the saying, 'If you can't say something nice, say nothing'?"

"Yes . . ."

"Well, this is a trial and you can't say nothing—therefore, you must say something nice!"

Gisella looked at the accused and remembered Flame's trial. How things had changed since then! Now she was the fox, hunting and killing what she could in order to live. She hadn't stolen any chickens . . . yet. But if she were hungry . . . ?

"Your Honor," she began, "I've seen many of the terrible things these two have done. But maybe they were simply doing the things that emperors and queens are supposed to do: waging wars, fighting for power, and grabbing everything they can; making history. Maybe they can't help it. Can a fox help hunting? Maybe they are like us foxes. And maybe they are just as innocent."

Was it true? All the pain, cruelty, destruction, and death,

maybe—like joy and love and beauty—maybe it was all just part of life. It was sad . . . but maybe it was no one's fault.

"The witness may step down," said the spider, and Gisella went back to her place.

"Any more witnesses for the defense?" asked the spider. "Friends? Family?"

"I had a friend," said the queen, "but she died. My family, too. Accidentally, of course!"

"Emperors don't have friends," said the emperor. "We have empires."

"Lawyer for the defense, your closing statement, please."

"Your Honor, birds of the jury," said Nubia, pacing again, scanning the room with his large yellow eyes. "What I am about to tell you may be very difficult—if not impossible—to believe; yet every word is true!" Nubia paused, then pointed dramatically at the defendants. "This emperor and this queen were the cutest, sweetest babies you ever saw. They liked being tickled and playing patty-cake. They ate up all their porridge, and when they were asleep, they looked like angels. The only thing they did wrong was to grow up! Is that a crime? Is there anyone here who hasn't done the same? Or won't do it when they get the chance? I rest my case."

Nubia returned to his place next to Gisella. "It was all I could think of," he whispered. The two rulers did look like angry children caught at being bad.

"Prosecution, your closing please." The owl-person person paced forward, arms—or were they wings?—folded behind him, his huge yellow eyes on the accused.

"Your Honor, birds of the jury: Are the emperor and the queen murderers and monsters? Or are they as innocent in their actions as the fox or the lion or the spider are in theirs? Is there evil in the world and are these two instruments of that evil? Or are they simply instruments of history? Should they be stopped? Should they be punished? The verdict is yours, but there isn't much time. The invisible world is vanishing. The magic is draining away. I know you will decide correctly. Thank you."

"This is utter nonsense!" cried the emperor. "It's you who will all be punished!"

"Severely punished!" echoed the queen.

A murmuring and chattering, a whispering and chittering whirled around the space overhead. The birds debated their decision.

"Your Honor," said the largest crow, "the jury has reached a verdict."

"How find you?" asked the spider.

"We find the accused to be—"

The doors flew open and there was a tremendous racketing roar and the smoke and smell of burning gasoline, and two huge motorcycles, each with a general on it, burst into the room. Gisella recognized the generals, one in black and the other in purple. They were followed by soldiers of both armies, rifles with bayonets at the ready.

"It's about time!" cried the emperor and queen. "Generals, destroy this circus!"

"Emperor Ignatz the XI, known as 'The Powerful,'" shouted the purple general in a voice like coughing and choking, "and Queen Sydnia, known as 'The Sweet,' you are both under arrest! Your stupid, wasteful war and corrupt policies have ruined all our countries! My former enemy, General Shmutz of the army of Surland, and I are taking over! We have formed new governments, with peace and justice for all! Now we are the law. Guards, take them away!"

The emperor and queen were dragged off protesting and cursing, and the generals and soldiers followed. Gisella looked up. She could see the sky overhead. The birds were gone. Would their verdict ever be known? Or maybe, she wondered . . . maybe what just happened was the verdict.

Except for Gisella and her little circus, and Tavido, Great-Aunt Tanteh, and her chickens, and, of course, Flame, the vast circular room was empty.

18

"Tavido," said Great-Aunt Tanteh. "Come here . . . come close." Tavido, tapping with his stick, turning his head this way and that, made his way across the mirrored crystal floor to her basket and knelt beside it. She kissed his forehead and pulled his ear close to her mouth. She whispered to him for a minute or so and put something into his hand. Tavido kissed her and smiled. His great-aunt smiled also.

"Now, my darlings," she said, "December and I must go." Her eyes glittered. "Gisella, come kiss me good-bye. . . ." Gisella ran to her.

"Great-Auntie, where are you going! Why must you go?" Gisella licked the old woman's face and rubbed against her cheeks with her muzzle, and she was kissed in return.

"You can't go," she said. "Stay! Please stay!"

"The magic is fading away," said the old woman, "far away. And I must follow. But as far as I go, I'll always be close, my little Gisella, to you. Don't worry. You'll find your happy ending."

They heard a loud honking. Gisella looked up and a gigantic gray goose glided through the window and across the room. It landed next to her, stretched its neck to Great-Aunt Tanteh, and they exchanged kisses. Then it took the basket by the handle with its beak and lifted it.

"Wait for me!" said April, fluttering into the basket. "I'm coming with you!"

"And I!" crowed Gabriel, joining them.

The great bird began to flap its wings and wind whirled around the room. The chandeliers tinkled and chimed. Slowly the goose rose with the basket, flew to the window, and then out it went, flapping into the sky. Great-Auntie smiled and waved as she and the chickens and basket and goose all grew smaller and smaller till they vanished into the blue. Far away.

Gisella called after them until she could no longer see them. There was so much she wanted to ask, so much only Great-Aunt Tanteh could tell.

"Gisehhh-laaaa . . ." Quick flew out of Gisella's ear and became himself. "Do you still need me, Gisella? May I go now and join my people? We must find a new world for ourselves. A new home . . . soon."

"Dear, brave Quick!" said Gisella. She knew she must let him go also. "You've saved us all. Bless you and thank you!"

"Good-bye, Gisella," he sang. "Good luck. . . ." His voice became the whirr of his hummingbird wings, and with a flash, he, too, was gone into the sky.

"Dear Gisella," said Tavido, picking her up and kissing her tears. "Even as a fox you are still my sister, my dear little sister whom I carried piggyback—but now it's time you had your own body again. Flame, come and look into her eyes . . . Flame?"

They looked around.

"She's gone!" cried Gisella.

"She ran off down the hall," said Nubia.

"My fiddle's gone, too!" said Tavido. "After her! Lead me by my stick!"

"I'll find her," growled the bear. "I'll get her!"

The bear and Nubia ran ahead, and Gisella guided Tavido through the mirrored corridors, out of the palace, and into the streets. They were full of people cheering and waving flags. The generals stood on a palace balcony overlooking the city. The purple general's voice, echoing from loudspeakers, boomed huge over the crowds: "A new day!" Cheering. "Freedom and Justice!" Cheering. "The tyrants will be punished!" Cheering.

Gisella and Tavido pushed through the crowds and ran back down the hills to the camp, where they met Nubia and the bear. The gates were open and the last few prisoners were limping through them down the road. Flame and Gisella's mother and grandfather were not among them. The sergeant was sitting in the little guardhouse, drinking a bottle of beer and eating a sausage. Gisella ran up to him, asking where her family had gone. He heard only barks and yelps and she realized they were no longer in the crossroads. Tavido couldn't understand her, either.

"You Crags have to clear out," said the sergeant to Tavido. "No Crags allowed in the country!"

"What about peace and justice for all?" asked Tavido.

"All except Crags," said the sergeant. Tavido asked about his family. "Oh, yes," the sergeant said. "The girl came back and told the others that Tavido—is that you?—would meet them at their farm in Surland. And off they went. But, of course, you can't stay in Surland, either."

"Where can we stay?" asked Tavido. The sergeant shrugged and went back to his sausage.

Tavido helped Nubia, the bear, and Gisella out of their circus clothes. It was bliss to be free of them. They all three rolled and squirmed on their backs in the dirt, groaning with pleasure. Then Gisella leapt up and began to run and the joy of freedom and movement took her flying around and past and over everything in her path; she couldn't imagine ever stopping. But finally, all at once, she was startled to remember Tavido and the others, and where they were going and what they had to do.

Gisella had to run a long way back to find them. Together, they crossed the border and headed for home.

19

The countryside was full of wandering Crag families, begging food and trying to find someplace they could stay. Many spoke of leaving the Old Country. There was talk of a land across the sea, a new world where it was said Crags were welcome, and where all the streets were paved with gold. Of course, Gisella didn't believe it. She had never seen a place where all the streets were paved.

As they traveled, Gisella and Nubia hunted food. The bear's leg had healed, with only a slight limp, and he foraged and hunted also. Gisella became a superb hunter. Almost nothing she turned her nose to escaped her.

One evening, on a hilltop, she'd lost the scent of a rabbit and she paused to find it. It was becoming autumn and the air itself was delicious and full of stories. Just breathing was like listening to music. Feelings of joy and longing and wonder washed through her. Life is hunting, she thought, and hunting is life. It amazed her that she had never understood this before.

They moved deeper into Surland, and the bear recognized his home woods. They followed one of his favorite trails and his spirits rose. He became more and more distracted by familiar scents and side trails.

"Gisella," he said, "we are in the land where I was born. I feel a longing to walk my old hills and smell my old caves and go about my own bear business, but if you still need my help. . . ."

"Dear bear," said Gisella. "I think that, between my brother, Nubia, and I, we can deal with Flame. Go your own way, and thank you for being with us."

"Good luck," said the bear, starting off. "Oh, and"—he stopped and turned—"please give Flame a message for me. . . ." Of course, Gisella would never repeat what he said next. She just laughed, and so did he, and then he disappeared among the trees.

One evening just as the sun was setting, they arrived at the place where their farm had been. Gisella didn't recognize it— the woods blasted away, craters everywhere, and the gaping, charred, stone-lined pit that was all that remained of her house. From the last limb of their now-dead oak, three bodies hung from stout ropes. There was a sign pinned to the one in the middle:

THIS WE DO TO THOSE
WHO OPPRESS CRAGS.
FIGHT FOR A CRAG HOMELAND!
—The New Crag Army—

Tavido couldn't see it, but after he understood that every-thing was gone, Gisella led him under the corpses, and he reached up and touched the leg of one and then another with his hand.

"Are they Crags?" he asked her. They had learned ways to talk to each other; she barked twice for no.

"Good!" he said with gritted teeth. "It's time we fought back! I will sleep here, on the ground underneath them. In the morning, you'll understand why." He lay down with a rock for a pillow, and Nubia and Gisella went off to hunt. There was nothing to catch. The fields and woods for miles around were dead. At dawn, they lay beside Tavido and waited for him to wake.

They were wet with the morning's dew by the time he stirred. He got to his feet and pulled off his bandage. Gisella winced. There were ugly scars where his eyes should have been. He reached overhead and took hold of the feet of the dead man hanging there. The corpse was also soaked with dew, and Tavido wet his hands with it and rubbed it over and into the scars. Then he sat down, eyes covered, and didn't move. Nubia and Gisella sat, too, and waited. After an hour or so, Tavido lowered his hands. He had eyes.

He squinted into the rising sun. He looked at Gisella and Nubia, and he laughed and wept and held them while Gisella laughed and wept, too.

"This is a gift from Great-Aunt Tanteh. Just before she left us, she told me that the dew from the body of a hanged man, if I spent the night under it, would restore my sight. And she also gave me this." From his pocket he took a golden egg. It glowed in the sunrise and lit a place on the trunk of the gallows tree under which they sat. There were words scratched into the bark:

> *Dear Tavido:*
>
> > *We have gone to the port to try somehow to work*
> > *or beg our way onto a ship to the New World.*
> > *We will wait there for you as long as we can.*
> > *God speed you to us.*
> >
> > > *Grandpa, Mother, and Gisella*

"After we get your body back, Gisella," said Tavido, "this egg will take you and Mother and Grandpa to the New World."

"What about you?" she asked him with her eyes and by licking him.

"I'm staying to fight." He pointed up to the sign on the corpse. "I'm joining the Crag army. When we have our own country, a place we can live and be free and safe, you'll all come back. Now, let's go! To the port!"

        ⋻   ⋻

It was another long journey. Gisella couldn't remember how many days or weeks, but on the way she became more and more restless and distracted. She felt she was looking for something; not her family or her body, something else, someone else. She didn't know what it was. One night, she woke to a sound she'd never heard before. It was a fox singing. A male fox. She sniffed the night and from a long way off, she caught his scent. A thrill rippled through her. Somehow, she knew he was singing to her, and it felt as if all her life she'd been waiting to hear his song. More than anything, she longed to sing back.

She woke Tavido and pressed herself to him. He heard the song, knew what it was, and understood.

"We'll be at the port soon, dear Gisella," he said, "soon." He held her through the night.

The next evening, they arrived at the port. It was a big, noisy, dirty city, with clanging streetcars. Gisella had to hide in the woods at the outskirts while Tavido and Nubia went to look for their family. The male fox's scent was in the air, and closer. Gisella tugged at Tavido's rope belt as he was leaving.

"You want me to tie you?" he asked. "So you can't run off to him?" She barked yes, and he tied her to a tree and left.

She sat listening to the song as night descended around her. The yearning she felt was like nothing she had ever felt before. Then she heard something moving toward her.

"Gisella," said a voice. It was Flame.

Gisella almost didn't recognize her. She looked older, paler, thinner. Now her voice was no longer Gisella's. It was Flame's.

"I have come," she said, "to give you back your body—even though I've become quite attached to it." She laughed. "You see how human I am? I know when I've made a joke. I've also become very attached to your family, your mother, grandfather, and Tavido, and I so miss Great-Aunt Tanteh; I'll be sorry to leave them all. And, of course, there's this. . . ." She took the fiddle out of a sack. "More than anything, I've longed to make music . . . like Tavido! Somehow, music is about the mystery of being human, and yet still being . . . wild. But I haven't been able to make it, no matter how I practice and try. Great-Aunt Tanteh was right; she told me that foxes can never make music until they've learned the magic that goes into it. Oh, yes! She knew all along I was a fox, and she cared for me anyway."

"What is the magic that makes music?" Gisella asked.

"It's something called love," said Flame. "I know less about it than I know about gold. But now they are going to cross the sea to the New World. The Old World's magic is draining away. It's now or never, Gisella. Take back your body, and your life, and—most of all—please forgive me, if you can, for the pain I've caused you."

Gisella looked at her and thought about her life as a fox— she had no idea how long it had been—all the strangeness and fear and struggle and, yes, pain. But there was joy, too, and beauty, and so many things she would never have known. And she sat down and Flame sat in front of her and Gisella told her all she had been through, all her adventures; it took quite a while. The stars glittered and the moon slid slowly down the sky. Flame listened. From time to time she smiled or laughed or shook her head. Sometimes tears fell.

"Dear Gisella," she said at last, "I am truly, deeply sorry. It was wrong of me to trick you . . . to take your body. Now I give you back what is yours." She looked into Gisella's fox eyes.

Gisella's mind raced. Which body was hers? Which life? Could she leave this place where she'd been born? Leave Tavido and the struggle he was beginning? Leave this poor broken, beaten, wounded Old Country that was trying to live again? And this fox body; she realized she'd come to take it for granted—its quickness, its grace, all the sounds and sights and smells only it could give her. The woods at midnight, the meadows at dawn. The hunt! Did she really want to leave it? She missed her mother and grandfather, but she had missed them for so long now, it was as if they were gone already into a new life that was theirs. She knew she would always love them, but she had a life that was hers. And out there, not far away, in what was left of the night, the he-fox was calling, coming closer.

Gisella took her eyes from Flame's. "Give my love to

Mother and Grandpa," she said, "and take good care of them. They will always be in my heart. I forgive you, and wish you well, Flame. I am a fox of the Old Country."

"Are you sure, Gisella?"

"Please," she said, "untie the rope." Flame did.

"I love you, Gisella," Flame said.

"I love you, Flame," said Gisella, and they looked at each other one last time. Then Flame turned and went off to the New World with Gisella's mother and grandfather.

When Tavido returned, he found the fox, his sister, gone.

POSTLUDE

‿❧ My Great-Granny Gisella, nodding slowly and with a slight smile, was silent. My mouth hung open. I looked at her, waiting for more. When I realized there was to be no more, I began to frown and shake my head.

"But . . . how . . . when . . . where did you finally change back? And come here to be my great-granny?"

"Gisella never did. I came. I, who was Flame the fox."

I stared at her, my eyes wide.

"If I had begun my story," the old woman continued, leaning closer, "by telling you I was born a fox, would you have listened? Would you have believed me?"

"Can I believe you now? Is it true?"

"The truth is the truth. What you can believe, that's up to you."

"You were really a fox?"

Great-Granny Gisella smiled and nodded. "It was in the Old Country," she said, as if that explained everything, "long, long ago. . . ."

"And what happened to . . . the real Gisella?"

"She met her he-fox, had a litter of cubs, and then another
. . . and another; all the while, she helped Tavido and the Crag
army. She was an excellent spy. Tavido wrote to me about her
in his letters when I got to this country. After some years—I
don't know how many—she disappeared into the woods. Into
the wild."

"And what happened to Tavido?"

"He became a leader of the Crags, and after years of struggle and fighting and prison, he and his comrades won. They
created a Crag republic where Crags live without fear. Of
course . . . if you happen to be a Surlander or Norlander, or
your mother was born in Outer Myopia, life isn't so good
there. He's an old man now, and at the moment, unfortunately, back in prison—politics, you know."

"And Nubia?"

"He gave up law and fathered many litters of kittens,
descendants of which still keep Tavido company."

"What about the emperor and queen, and those two
generals?"

"The emperor and queen were both executed, and shortly
after, one of the generals, I don't remember which, pushed the
other off the balcony during a speech and made himself dicta-
tor, which he remained for many years, till the sergeant took
over. Remember the sergeant? Now they're supposed to have

some kind of democracy . . . I'm not sure. But someday you must go there and visit the amazing Crystal Palace! It's open to the public Wednesdays and Sundays, if it's not closed for repairs."

"And Quick?"

"Quick and his people are gone to where we can never find them, except in stories. We are poorer for losing them as neighbors."

"And you and your . . . ?"

"Stepmother and Stepgrandpa?"

"Yes! And the golden egg?"

"After a long, stormy voyage, we reached these shores, and Grandpa used the golden egg to buy a little delicatessen, which became very famous for its Crag-style sausages, not to mention the cinnamon honey cake. They made enough money for violin lessons, and as you know, I eventually learned to play quite well."

"And the magic . . . from the invisible world; is it really all gone?"

"No. It's harder to find, but there's still some left . . . I see some in your eyes." She paused. A slow smile came over her face. "I have one last thing for you," she said.

From a pocket she took a little battered tin box and gave it to me. It looked old and foreign. My fingers trembled as I pulled off the tight lid. Inside, wrapped in a piece of black velvet, was a fragment of what looked like eggshell, except that it was gold. I stared at it, and then at Great-Granny.

"And what about me?" I whispered. "What does all this . . . make me?"

"You are my dear great-grandchild. This story I've told you, it's not just mine. It's yours, also."

Great-Granny Gisella smiled, and nodded slowly.

That's how I will always remember her.